DRAGON'S DESIRE

THE DRAGON SHIFTER'S MATES

EVA CHASE

INK SPARK PRESS

Dragon's Desire

Book 3 in the Dragon Shifter's Mates series

First Digital Edition, 2017

Cover design: Another World Designs

Ebook ISBN: 978-0-9959865-9-6

Paperback ISBN: 978-1-989096-00-0

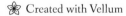 Created with Vellum

CHAPTER 1

Ren

SOMETIMES YOU GET a moment so heavenly you can hardly believe this really is your life. Like falling asleep cuddled between four insanely hot alpha shifters who are destined to be your mates.

A few weeks ago, I hadn't even been dating anyone. I'd only just gotten myself an actual apartment. Now I was enveloped in protective affection—and let's not forget the hotness—on the biggest, softest bed I'd ever seen in an estate so impressive it took my breath away. Okay, so more than a few people had tried to kill me in the last several days, but as I'd drifted off to sleep I was feeling like on the whole I'd come out ahead.

But of course, those heavenly moments never last. Something always shatters them. This time? It was a knock on the door in the middle of the night and a quavering voice saying, "There's been an attack on the bear alpha's estate."

West, who'd answered the door, flicked on the light in the sitting room. The wolf shifter's voice came out tight. "I think you'd better come in."

The rest of us were already clambering off the bed. I'd been so exhausted that night I hadn't bothered changing. My dress from the farewell party with the avian shifters hung on me in a mess of wrinkles. I gave the soft fabric a quick tug and rubbed my eyes as I hustled to the doorway.

Aaron, the alpha of the avian kin and current owner of this estate, strode ahead of me. The light glanced off his golden hair the same way the sun shone off his feathers in his majestic eagle form. I'd always thought of him as my Disney prince, but right now his blue eyes were sharp and his square jaw clenched. More warrior than royalty.

"What exactly happened?" he asked the attendant who'd come with the message.

Nate, my massive bear shifter, came up beside Aaron. His usual gentle presence had fallen away, aggressive tension radiating from his brawny body. "Is anyone hurt?" he demanded in his low baritone. "Who attacked my people?"

West leaned against the wall by the door, his arms crossed over his lean chest and his green eyes narrowed. Marco, the jaguar shifter who was alpha to the feline kin, stopped beside me and set his hand on my shoulder tentatively. He and I hadn't exactly been on the best of terms in the last couple days—his fault, for shooting off his mouth to his kin and talking about me like I was some kind of prize to compete over—but now we clearly had bigger concerns.

The attendant ducked his head, his hands clasped in front of him. "I only know that we received an urgent call. The staff on the estate hope that their alpha can return as quickly as possible. It appears a group of rogue shifters somehow managed to break into the estate and attempted a surprise attack on some of the advisors and their families."

A growl rumbled from Nate's chest. "I'll go now."

"We'll all go," I said. "We were going to head there in the morning anyway. That's probably why they picked your estate to attack."

We all knew that the attack had probably been more about me than any of my alphas or their kin. As the last dragon shifter alive, it was my role not just to take all four of the alphas as my mates but to unite the entire shifter community at the same time. Given that I hadn't even known shifters existed, let alone that I was one, until a few weeks ago, I had a lot of work ahead of me.

But I wasn't going to back down. Especially not when it came to the assholes who'd killed my fathers and sisters.

Nate gave me a quick nod, already hustling out the door. For a guy that big, he could move awfully fast when he needed to. The rest of us hurried out behind him.

"Find whatever pilot is most rested," Aaron instructed the attendant. "We'll take the jet."

"The jet?" I repeated. I'd missed that part of the estate, apparently.

"Each of the estates has a couple of private jets on hand in case we or our advisors need to take care of matters elsewhere in a hurry," he explained as we headed down the white-walled hall. "It's a lot more reliable than counting on human-arranged flights."

"It just seems a little strange. Here, anyway. I mean, all of you can fly already."

The corner of his mouth quirked up into a tense smile. "Not half as fast as an airplane, even on my best days."

Fair. I wasn't sure I could beat a jet even in my dragon form. And I couldn't hold my dragon form for more than fifteen minutes so far, so that was kind of a moot point anyway.

We'd just burst through a side door into the warm summer night when another set of footsteps pattered behind us. Alice, Aaron's younger sister and self-appointed bodyguard, dashed to join us. Her golden-blond hair was pulled back in a sleek ponytail and her eyes were brightly alert. Did the girl ever sleep?

"I heard the news," she said. "This time I'm coming along."

"Alice," Aaron started.

She waved her finger at him. "Nope. No arguments this time. Last time you were just going on a little trip to maybe find a missing dragon shifter, and you ended up battling rogues and nearly getting poisoned by faeries. This time we *know* someone where you're going wants you dead. Who knows what the hell other trouble you'll all get into?"

Aaron didn't look convinced, but he also didn't look like he had the energy to argue. It was still completely dark out. We couldn't have slept for more than a couple hours. And yesterday had been a very long day.

"I want Alice with us," I piped up to make his agreement easier. "It'll be nice to have a little break from all the testosterone."

West muttered something under his breath, and Marco chuckled. A twinge of guilt pinched my stomach. It was my best friend Kylie, who was back in Brooklyn recovering from a rogue attack right now, I should have been counting on for girl talk. But our friendship had gotten a little more complicated with every strange and scary revelation I'd encountered.

Alice grabbed my hand and gave it a squeeze in thank you. And I guessed to reassure me, because then she leaned over and said, "It'll be okay. We've handled worse."

I wasn't sure if that actually made me feel better. The shifter community had faced an awful lot of problems in the years they'd gone without a dragon shifter. It wasn't my fault that my mom had gone on the run and decided to lock away my memories of what I was, but it was hard not to feel a little responsible for the mess she'd left behind. I was the only one left who could pull the pieces back together.

The salty breeze off the Pacific washed over us as we loped along a path between a stretch of trees. On the other side, a small plane waited on a grassy runway. We scrambled up the steps into the cabin.

The space was bigger than I'd have expected from the outside of the plane. The ceiling was high enough that even Nate didn't need to hunch. Five pairs of leather-cushioned seats lined one wall. Marco dropped into one, running his hand through his jagged black hair. Aaron went to talk to the pilot who'd come running over.

It was a good thing the ceiling could accommodate Nate, because he was pacing back and forth in the aisle. His jaw worked and his hands were balled at his sides. "When I find them," he said. "When I find the rogues who did this..."

"Hey." I touched his arm, and he stopped, turning toward me. I looked up at him, raising my hand to cup his cheek. "We *will* find them, and we'll make them regret any harm they've done. We're getting there as fast as we can."

"I know. I just—" He shook his head. Teasing his fingers into my hair, he bent to kiss me. The tender press of his lips gave me the same shiver of pleasure as always, but I could still feel the frustration coiled through his body. He wasn't going to be able to relax until we got to his estate.

"This might help," Aaron said, returning. He tossed a cell phone to Nate and passed two others to West and Marco. "One of my assistants grabbed them from your rooms. The pilot is just checking the systems. We should be ready to go in a minute."

Nate grasped the phone with a relieved exhale and dialed a number. He went back to pacing as he brought the phone to his ear. I wavered on my feet, not sure what to do now. Was there anything I *could* do? I hated feeling this useless.

The jet's engine thrummed on. A hand grasped my wrist. "I don't think you want to try takeoff standing up,

Sparks," West said in his usual gruff tone. He tugged me toward the seat next to him. "That might be a little much even for you."

I rolled my eyes at him. "Thanks for your concern." But I did sit down. West and I currently had a... very complicated relationship. He insisted he still wasn't sure I was cut out for the dragon shifter's role—or the role of his mate. On the other hand, he'd seemed very enthusiastic about me when we'd made out the other night. The earth and pine smell of him next to me was enough to get me a little warm between the legs as I remembered that moment.

At least the last time we'd talked he'd been able to admit that his issues were mostly his, not mine. And every now and then I saw a softer side to him. He'd stood up for me when I needed it. Thrown himself into battle more than once to protect me. The rest I guessed we'd just have to take it as it came.

Even Nate had finally sat down now, although he was talking urgently into the phone. The rumble of the engine rose as the jet started to move. It hurtled forward with increasing speed. There was a quick jolt, and we lifted off the ground.

My stomach lurched, but I knew it wasn't just because of the acceleration. The rogues had already caused enough pain in my life. The last thing I was looking forward to was seeing the destruction they'd brought to Nate's estate.

CHAPTER 2

Ren

THE PLANE SHUDDERED, and my eyes popped open. I hadn't even realized I'd closed them, but they were so heavy I'd obviously been asleep for a while. There was a crick in my neck from having my head slumped over.

Slumped over against... someone's leanly muscled shoulder. A shoulder that held the faint scent of earthy pine.

Oh crap. I jerked back in my seat, my heart skipping. I'd been so tired from our late and then interrupted night that I'd fallen asleep on my neighbor. Who happened to be West.

Who was watching me with an unreadable expression now.

"Um, sorry about that," I said. "I promise I didn't do it on purpose. I would never mistake you for a pillow."

Maybe that wasn't the most solid apology ever? I

could definitely read the wolf shifter's expression now: That, folks, was a glower.

"Somehow that didn't stop you from using me as one," he pointed out.

"Yeah, well, you know, unconscious and all, can't be held responsible for my actions." I gestured vaguely with my hands.

"I hope that's not an excuse you're planning on pulling out very often."

I rolled my eyes. Would it kill him to cut me a break for a minute here and there? "If it bothered you so much, you could always have woken me up and made me move."

Something shifted in West's eyes. Something that made my mind trip back to that moment in the garden the other night when he'd laid me beneath him on that bench, his mouth all over me. I'd swear the temperature between us rose by ten degrees in that one instant as he held my gaze now, but maybe it was only me feeling it.

He reached out and grazed his fingers over my cheek. Brushing an errant strand of my hair away from my eyes. My pulse hiccupped at the gentle touch. He was so close it would have been simple to tangle my fingers in his silver-streaked auburn hair and—

West sat back in his seat, turning his gaze toward the front of the plane. Away from me. "We're almost there. Better prepare yourself, Sparks. Your job is only going to get harder."

I mentally smacked myself. Even if West had been remotely receptive to some kind of come on, now wasn't the time to be thinking about getting it on with anyone.

We had the rogue attack to deal with. I still didn't know how serious the assault had been.

It was just hard to ignore the unceasing tug of the bond inside me. I was pretty sure the pull was getting even more insistent when it came to the two guys I hadn't consummated our bond with yet. Apparently *it* didn't care that I had perfectly good reasons for taking my time with Marco and West.

I leaned to the other side of my seat. It was easy to spot Nate a couple rows up. His dark brown hair, thick as his grizzly bear pelt, showed over the back of his seat. He had at least a few inches on all the other guys, all of whom were far from short.

My hand dropped to my seatbelt. But before I could go over and ask what the bear shifter had found out with his phone calls, the plane jerked again. A calm voice filtered from the speaker on the ceiling.

"You all should remain seated for the next ten minutes. We're coming in for our landing now."

Okay, I guessed I wasn't going anywhere yet. I tried to relax in my seat, but my heart was thumping now, and that had nothing to do with West a few inches away beside me. A glance out the window showed a stretch of rocky, desert-like landscape bleeding into a dense forest in the thin light of the emerging dawn. Nate's estate—the center of operations for the disparate kin who didn't belong to the canine, feline, or avian groups—lay in one of the wilder parts of California.

And because they'd known I was coming there, the rogues had gone after his advisors. *And* their families. If any children had been hurt because of me...

My chest tightened, and my fingers curled around the armrests. No. I couldn't think like that. I was doing my best. Any violence committed was totally on the rogues. If they had such a big problem with dragon shifters, they could have brought it up peacefully.

I knew all that, but it didn't completely loosen the twist of guilt around my heart.

My ears had started to pop with the change in air pressure when my phone chimed with a text alert. I wriggled it out of the pocket of my jeans. It had to be Kylie. At least talking to my best friend would take my mind off whatever disaster was waiting for us down there while I couldn't do anything to fix it yet.

Hey, girl. Didn't hear from you yesterday, just wanted to make sure you survived that big to-do the other night. And that they survived your gorgeousness in that dress!!!

Shit, had I really not talked to her at all yesterday? Between an assassination attempt, a confrontation with the faerie monarch, and the farewell party, I'd hardly had a chance to breathe. But Kylie had no idea what might have been going on here. Whether I might have found myself in more trouble. I hadn't told her the more dire parts of my adventures, but she'd seen the danger that could come with my role before I'd insisted she stay behind. Along with the rogue attack that had left her clawed up, she'd witnessed a skirmish between my alphas and a bunch of vampires.

Now I had double the guilt weighing on me. I quickly typed an answer. *Sorry! Crazy day. Yes, everyone survived the dress, including me. We just left for Nate's estate in California.*

Oh, wow, Cali! You definitely have to invite me over there sometime once you've settled in. That's at the top of my States To Visit list.

I smiled. *Of course. Right now, though... Probably not the best time.* I hesitated, debating how much to tell her. *You know the guys who attacked us in the shifter village? Some other rogues from their group broke into the estate last night.*

Oh, shit. Is everyone down there okay?

I don't know yet. But I'm definitely glad you're back in Brooklyn away from all the chaos.

Kylie sent back an emoji blowing a kiss. *You know I'd have your back no matter what, no matter where, Ren. Just say the word, and I'm there.*

I did know that. That was exactly why I wasn't telling her about the recent attempt on my life. It meant a lot to me that Kylie cared about me that much—until I'd met my alphas, she'd been the only person other than my mom who had—but I didn't want to put her in any more danger than I already had.

I started to text back asking what she'd been up to when the plane took a sharper dip. My seat vibrated as the wheels hit the runway. Stones rattled against the jet's undercarriage. It slowed to a halt almost immediately.

My gut knotted. We were here.

Sorry, I wrote to Kylie. *I've got to go now. Shifter business. I'll catch up with you more later.*

Don't worry about me! she replied with a line of hearts. As if I could help worrying.

But for now I was definitely more worried about what was waiting for us on the estate. Seatbelts clicked open all through the plane. We hustled out of our seats and down the steps.

The dry, hard-packed earth of the runway was lined with tall redwoods. Their tangy smell washed over me along with the chirping of an insect chorus.

A contingent of shifters I assumed were Nate's kin had come out to meet us. They were definitely a varied bunch. A muddle of scents tickled my nose as we approached the group. My dragon senses identified them on instinct: black bear, stoat, mink, elk, armadillo, manatee.

Nervous energy wafted off them, easing slightly when they saw their alpha in our midst. Nate strode to the head of our group, his jaw set and his eyes dark. But his kin's gazes drifted away from him to settle on me. A prickle traveled over my skin.

When I'd met some of West's canine kin in one of their villages, and when I'd arrived at the avian estate, almost all of the shifters had been friendly. Not just friendly, actually—they'd seemed awed to be in my presence. Fawning over me, wanting to touch me and hear me speak. It'd been a little overwhelming.

I couldn't say I missed the pressure of that kind of welcome. But this one... I wasn't sure these shifters were even happy I was here. Their eyes seemed to evaluate me as I came to a stop beside my newly consummated mate. Nate rested a hand on my back in acknowledgement, but his attention was completely on his kin.

"You made it here quickly," said the black bear shifter, a shorter but equally burly man who looked to be around forty. His short black hair stood up in a high buzz-cut. "It's good to have you back."

"We came as soon as we heard," Nate said. "Anything new to report, Thomas?"

Thomas started to walk down a path that I assumed led farther into the estate. The rest of us followed. Alice fell into step between me and Aaron as if she were trying to maximize her chances of protecting both of us. Her sharp eyes roved the forest.

"The current count is nine kin with major injuries, four dead," the black bear shifter said, his voice rough as he gave the numbers. "How many with scratches and bruises, we didn't bother to count."

Nate rubbed his mouth, grimacing. "Who did we lose?"

"The rogues were clearly targeting the wing where the advisors reside. They broke into Yvonne's and Garret's rooms first, before there'd even been much time to sound the alarm. And they had weapons—a few guns, the other ones knives... All of us put up as good a fight as we could, but Garret fell, and Yvonne's mate. And two of the guards who intervened."

"How did they get in?" Marco piped up. "I've seen the walls you've got around this compound. And I assume some of the guards were guarding those."

Thomas's voice dropped to almost a growl. He didn't like anyone but his alpha questioning him, I got the impression. "We're not sure yet how they got in. We *do* patrol the grounds carefully, especially after hearing about recent problems, but none of the guards saw the intruders until after they were already at the estate house."

"I'm sure everyone here was doing their job with their full ability," Nate said. "The rogues have been turning to tricks that no shifter should lower themselves to. What happened to the attackers?"

We emerged from the path into a tiled courtyard. Our feet rapped against the polished slabs of clay. A huge adobe mansion that I had to guess was the "estate house" Thomas had mentioned loomed at one end of the yard. Kneeling figures were scattered across its steps and in the hallway beyond its open, arched doorway.

"We killed most of them in the struggle," Thomas said. "The way they came at us, with no concern for themselves—they almost forced us to. It was a bloody night, I can tell you that much."

We came up to the steps, his last words rolling through my mind, and I realized what all those kneeling shifters were doing. They were scrubbing at the tiles and the walls with rags. Scrubbing at ruddy patches that dappled the clay and the pale brown adobe.

Blood. All that shifter blood spilled here last night...

Suddenly all the blood in my own body seemed to be rushing past my ears with the thudding of my heart. My vision swam.

There had been blood—blood everywhere. Blood splattering the walls painted in the delicate shade of yellow my mother had let my sisters and me pick out. Blood pooled under my wolf-father's slumped form. Blood gushing from the bullet wounds in my oldest sister's chest. The boom of more shots echoing down the hall. My mother's hand so tight around mine the bones pinched. The frantic patter of my feet down the hardwood floor.

The smell of it. Thick and metallic, saturating the air, mingling with the harsh smoky scent of the guns. It had trickled down my throat and filled my stomach, until my gut twisted and heaved—

No, heaving was happening now. I stumbled and bent down, clutching my belly. My pulse rattled painfully. The memories kept streaming through my head, the horrible smell sixteen years gone clogging my nose.

Temperance, my oldest sister, the one who'd always encouraged me to climb higher, run faster, even when I faltered. She'd shoved me out of the way as the rogues had opened fire through the doorway. And Verity, just two years older than me—Mom had tried to grab us both. That was when my eagle shifter father had thrown himself at the rogue with the rifle, talons gouging and wings shielding us. The bullets of a pistol had torn right through him, and she—and she—

"Ren," someone was saying. "Ren!" A strong arm had wrapped around my trembling back.

A sob caught in my throat. Nate's musky peppery smell followed it, chasing away the phantom scents from my past. I grasped his shirt, clinging on to him as if he were the only thing keeping me in place. At that moment, maybe he was.

I wasn't in the dragon shifter's estate. I wasn't five years old anymore. I focused on the clay tiles under my feet, the warm breeze, the quiet murmurs around us—

Shit. I shoved myself upright with a quick swipe at my eyes. Nate kept his arm around me, which was probably a good thing, because my legs wobbled for a second before I found my balance. Aaron was standing at my other side, Alice right in front of me. She touched my shoulder, her tone light but her eyes concerned.

"Hey. Are you okay?"

"Yeah," I said, willing my voice to stay steady. "I'm sorry. I didn't expect— It just reminded me of the attack on my mother's—on my estate. When I was a kid. When —" My throat started to close up. Better not to go into any more detail than that. From the look on Alice's face, she already understood what I meant.

And beyond her, the delegation of Nate's kin who'd come out to meet us, the shifters working at washing away the mess of last night's attack, they were all watching me. Watching me make a total fool of myself. How the hell were they going to trust that I could deal with this threat when just seeing the aftermath sent me halfway to a breakdown? My hands clenched.

"I'm okay," I said firmly, squaring my shoulders.

"Your memories were suppressed for so long, it's understandable that you're not used to handling the more traumatic ones," Aaron said. I wondered how much that reassurance was for my benefit and how much for the other shifters.

"Well, I'll just have to get used to handling them," I said. "Right now we have to focus on the attack that happened *here*, and how we can make sure it doesn't happen again."

Thomas made a soft coughing sound. He directed his

gaze at his alpha. "On that topic... I said we had to kill *most* of the rogues in the assault. But we did manage to capture one—and to stop him before he could end his own life. We had to subdue him with a tranquilizer for the time being, but we can wake him up when you're ready to question him."

CHAPTER 3

West

WE KIN groups had plenty of differences between us. There was no denying that. But at the core, in some vital ways, we were the same. A shifter kin funeral looked and sounded like a shifter kin funeral whether the dead being honored were canine or feline or avian—or something else, like today.

All the shifters who lived on the estate had gathered around the massive pyre. The sharp smell of fresh sap nearly overwhelmed the stink of death. Four bodies lay there to be laid to rest. Their loved ones had come forward to talk about the lives of the fallen. Now Nate was moving from one body to the next, flames hissing on the end of the torch he carried. His low baritone voice swept through the clearing.

"Brother of my heart, kin to your alpha. Your light has snuffed out, but now you will burn brighter. As we let you go, we swear to rise up stronger for you."

"We swear to rise up stronger," a chorus of voices rang out around the pyre. I added mine to it. A few bodies down from me, Ren startled and managed to join in for the last few words.

Just one more thing our dragon shifter didn't know about her own kind.

She'd missed the funeral for her own fathers and sisters. The massive one kin from all across the country had arrived for. I'd only been eleven, but I remembered starkly the sight of the alpha before me, the man who'd mentored me for the past three years, lying limp and vacant on the heap of firewood. The bullet hole marring his skin had looked so unnatural, like some horrible disease and not a proper battle wound.

The rogues were fucking unnatural, the way they slaughtered their own kind for their selfish reasons. I gritted my teeth, thinking about the one Nate's guards had managed to capture. Wouldn't I like to be sinking those teeth into him right now. If we hadn't needed the information he could give us, I'd like to tear out his throat for what he'd done here. For what they'd done back then. For all of it, really.

"We swear to rise up stronger," we repeated for the fourth time. Nate bowed his head. Then he tossed his torch onto the pyre.

The flames crackled, sweeping over the heap of woods and the bodies lying on it in a wave. Smoke billowed up. It prickled into my eyes and down my throat, coating my tongue. And the memory that rose up then wasn't of my mentor.

How many bodies had we sent back to the light the

day I'd said good-bye to my mother? Eight. Eight loyal kin felled. I'd had to order my people to build two pyres to hold them all. My throat had been hoarse by the time I'd finished the rounds. One of my advisors had offered to share the duty, seeing as I was fifteen and not yet fully of age, but I'd told him no. It'd been my battle. The deaths had been dealt because of my decisions.

I'd just had to believe we'd have seen more deaths if my decisions had been different.

Dad hadn't believed that. Or maybe he hadn't cared. The memory of his turned back, his shoulders stubbornly stiff, had stopped stinging over the years, even though he still hadn't said a word to me since. I was his alpha, but I wasn't his son anymore.

Today, it took a long time for the flames to burn down. We stood in silent witness the entire time, letting the smoke and the smell wash over us. Honoring to our dead.

Normally when the last flames flickered out amid the embers, we would see the ashes carried to their resting place and then be done. But when Nate stirred to move forward, Ren touched his arm. She stepped out from our ring toward the foot of the pyre.

Her face still looked a little paler than usual, making her dark eyes and hair gleam starkly in contrast. But I had to admire the strength with which she held herself, the steadiness of her posture. Whatever memories had rocked her when we'd arrived this morning, she'd wrestled them under control.

Her voice came out steady too—steady and clear.

"The rogues have gotten away with too much, for too

long. I wish I could have been here sooner to fulfill my role as dragon shifter. But now that I am here, I swear to you that we will see justice for these deaths. And if I have my way, the rogues won't shed one more drop of kin blood."

She raised a fist in the air and snapped it back to her side. A solemn air still hung over the gathering, but several voices in the crowd rose up in agreement. "Not one more drop!"

I bit back a frown. I wished I could cheer too, but our dragon shifter wasn't in any position to be giving her word on that matter. Her mother hadn't been able to take on the rogues, and she'd been a dragon shifter with years of experience, who'd grown up into the role. The fact that Ren would even try to make that kind of promise just showed how much she still had to learn.

Maybe the times really had changed. Maybe there were things a dragon shifter couldn't set right anymore, even with new powers and the four of us by her side.

Well, I hadn't committed myself yet, as much as parts of me had wanted to. It wasn't her fault she was so far behind, but that didn't mean I had to sacrifice myself and my kin holding her up.

I told myself that, but at the same time the determination on her face tugged at my heart. That damned mate bond still nagging at me, stirring up my emotions. I had to keep a tighter leash on them. If one touch from her could sever all my self-control, how could I put my kin first?

~

Ren

The pungent scent of the fire's smoke followed me down into the basement of Nate's estate house. I rubbed at my bare arms and resisted the urge to clear my throat. Would that be some kind of sign of disrespect? There were so many shifter traditions and expectations I still didn't know.

And from the way West had narrowed his eyes at me as we'd left the funeral clearing, he was keeping a careful tally of them.

Thankfully my other three alphas and Alice weren't looking for excuses to dismiss me. We had a rogue to interrogate—one who hopefully knew more than the avian woman who'd attacked me on Aaron's estate had. She'd been forced to cooperate. This one had joined the fight right alongside the others.

The guard who'd led us down to the short row of holding cells nodded to one room. On the other side of the door's small window, a skinny man with scruffy light brown hair was slumped on a bench. His wrists and ankles were chained to opposite ends, so he couldn't hurt us—or himself. As long as he was in human form, at least.

I stepped back from the window. "How do we know he won't shift to get out of the shackles?"

"The tranquilizer we use in situations like this suppresses the ability to shift," Aaron said, ready as ever with explanations. "The guards will have lowered the dose so he's conscious enough to talk to us, but his bodily control is still inhibited."

"He should be awake enough now," the guard said. He unlocked the door for us.

Nate strode in first, anger radiating off him. Marco slipped in ahead of me. As I passed through the doorway, my nose caught the rogue's scent. He was canine—some sort of dog. I wasn't surprised. He had the look of a mutt.

West's teeth bared when he came in. For once his glare was turned on someone other than me. This guy would have been his kin if the dog shifter hadn't turned to murder instead.

Aaron stayed in the doorway, Alice right behind him. She stood tensed, as if she didn't totally believe the precautions taken would be enough to protect us.

"You," Nate growled. "Let's start with the easy questions. What's your name?"

The dog shifter's gaze slid up toward Nate's face, but his thin lips stayed clamped tight. He swayed slightly where he sat, his shoulders hunched.

Nate loomed even higher over him. "I don't want to hurt anyone," he said. "But I've just come back from sending off four of my kin, whose deaths *you* had a hand in. I've got nine others still recovering. So I'm not feeling very forgiving at the moment. We can do this the painful way if you want."

"I have nothing to say to you," the rogue spat out. His voice was slightly slurred, I guessed because of the tranquilizer.

My back stiffened. If he'd attacked us, I'd have had no problem seeing Nate savage him. And there was no question in my mind that he deserved payback. But if what we wanted was answers, I wasn't sure torture was going to get us any. We'd watched rogues throw themselves to their deaths, impale themselves on our claws, just to avoid talking. They didn't seem to value their own lives much compared to their cause.

"I'll ask you again," Nate said, his tone turning even darker. He raised his hand, and it shifted into a giant grizzly bear paw. "Just tell us your name."

The rogue stared back with a wavering but defiant gaze. Words tumbled from my mouth before I'd even thought them through.

"There's another way we can get him talking. I can use the truth-seeking flames. It worked on the fae monarch."

Nate turned to me. "Are you sure you're up for that, Ren?"

I shrugged. Now that I'd volunteered, I'd better be. "I've had a day to get my energy back. And it'll be a lot faster than anything else we could try. You know what the rogues are like."

"Yes." He eyed the dog shifter. The rogue stayed where he was with the same hunched posture, but I thought a little of the remaining color in his yellowed face might have drained away. He might not know what I was talking about, but he knew it probably wasn't good for him.

That settled things. "Let's do it. Now, while the tranquilizer is still affecting him. We'll need to bring him to a bigger space so I have room to shift."

"That can be arranged." Nate motioned to the guard.

The rest of us backed out of the room. "You'll have to ask most of the questions," I said to the other alphas. "I can't carry on much of a conversation while I'm busy spewing flames."

"I think we can handle that, Princess," Marco said with a grim smile. He brought his hands together, one clapping over the other in a fist. "There are an awful lot of things I'd like to find out from that asshole."

Nate and his guard marched the rogue out of the cell, Nate holding the chains for the prisoner's left arm and leg and the guard those for the right. The dog shifter walked sluggishly. He glanced over his shoulder at me with a flash of the whites of his eyes. Nervous.

We tramped back up the stairs. Just as we reached the hall, the rogue wrenched at his arms. He threw himself forward and around, putting all his strength into breaking his captors' hold.

Fortunately for us, Nate and his guard had plenty of strength on their side, and the rogue's was muted by the drug. Nate wrestled the dog shifter still with a quick jerk of the chains. Alice stepped closer, her hands fisted.

"You can walk, or we can carry you," Nate said. "Your choice."

The rogue grimaced at him. Then he started walking again.

Our strange procession took a sharp turn and ended up out behind the estate house in a small yard of hard-packed earth and tufts of grass. "This field is usually for outdoor sports and training," Nate told me over his shoulder. "We'll have plenty of room. And we can make use of this."

He hauled the rogue over to a rectangle of metal

jutting out of the earth. A mini-sized football goal, I realized after a moment.

Nate and the guard attached the chains to the sturdy posts. The rogue tugged at his bindings, but only feebly. Then he shrank down as close to the ground as he could get in a cringing pose. I guessed he'd given up.

I walked up to him until I was just a few feet away. He just looked at the ground.

"I won't be doing this to torture you, but I don't get the impression it feels all that great either," I said. "If you want to skip that part, you could start answering questions now. Tell us why you and your 'friends' attacked this estate."

Not a peep.

Fine. We'd do this the dragon way.

I backed up a couple steps to make sure I didn't trample him as I shifted. With a nonchalance that was becoming easier every time I had to do this, I pulled off my shirt and kicked off my pants. I'd already ruined enough clothes with impromptu shifts over the last few weeks. The warm evening air washed over my bare skin. I leaned forward and let myself fall into the shift.

Reaching down and bringing forth the dragon side of me was coming easier every time too. I didn't have to struggle at all now. The scales and talons were waiting just on the other side of my skin, itching to break free. I opened myself up to them, and, with an exhilarating tingling, my dragon shape expanded through my body.

Literally. My neck extended, my eyes sharpening, my teeth rising into points. My limbs steadied beneath my lengthening torso. A barbed tail lashed out behind me,

27

and vast wings sprouted from my back. I stretched them over me, taking a little of the edge off the urge to soar up into the sky. I wasn't needed up there right now. My business was right here on the ground.

Flames tickled the base of my throat. A deeper heat filled my dragon lungs. I dragged in a breath, sensing the difference between the two flames I could cast down. The scorching destructive burn of my usual dragon fire—and the bright, crisp blaze that could cut through to the truth. As much as part of me wanted to unleash the first for what the dog shifter had done here, it was the second I drew into my mouth.

With a hot gush, I let those violet flames pour down over the rogue.

A yelp broke from his throat. He thrashed at his chains, an incoherent mumbling spilling past his lips.

For a second I thought my power hadn't worked. That somehow this mangy shifter had enough will to resist where even the queen of the fae hadn't. Then his mouth burst wide open to answer my earlier request.

"We knew the dragon shifter was coming here with all of the alphas," the rogue gasped out. "The kin-groups are starting to rally. We had to show that even with the alphas united, we rogues have more power. We can destroy you if we want. The alphas no longer get to call all the shots. They have to bend to *our* will."

Yeah, we'd see about that. As my flames streamed on down, Nate stepped forward, his arms crossed over his brawny chest. "Are there more of your group nearby? Are they planning another attack?"

"There's a large bunch of us gathering in the south. I

don't know exactly where. I wasn't told, so that I couldn't tell you. And we'll keep attacking until the alphas and the dragon shifters no longer control shifter kind."

"What exactly do you think is going to be so great about *that* situation?" Marco put in.

A whine crept into the dog shifter's voice. "I don't know. I haven't really thought about it much. But I don't like that we all have to kowtow to your rules, and everyone who doesn't is kept on the outside. If there were no alphas, we'd all be the same, making our own rules."

Somehow I didn't think it'd happen exactly like that. Whoever was in charge of the rogue group, they must be awfully persuasive.

An uncomfortable prickling was starting to fill my lungs. I couldn't sustain these flames for much longer. I scraped my talons against the ground in what I hoped the alphas would realize was a warning.

"How many of you are there still?" Aaron asked quickly.

"Maybe twenty that I've met. Dozens of rogues throughout the country. We recruit more of them every day." The dog shifter clutched his head, shaking it but unable to stay silent.

"What do you have planned as your next moves?" West said.

"I don't know. We don't know our instructions until right before we act."

My chest was outright aching now. I aimed one final blast of violet fire at the rogue, and Nate got in one last question.

"How did you get past the guards to break into the estate?"

The rogue chuckled. Actually *chuckled*, as if the question was funny. "Oh," he said. "We didn't have any trouble there. We had someone happy to help us. A raccoon shifter named Keith—one of the guards. He let us right in, your precious kin did."

CHAPTER 4

Ren

THE TRUTH-SEEKING FLAMES drained me faster than any of my other shifter powers. I tried to hold on a few seconds longer, to give my alphas a chance to push the rogue for more answers, but my body crumpled. The fire snapped out. I collapsed in on myself, into my human form.

Aaron was at my side in an instant, handing me my clothes. His jaw was tight. As I reached for my shirt, Nate lunged past us. He shifted into his grizzly form, charging up to the rogue.

The dog shifter recoiled instinctively. But when Nate opened his jaws threateningly, he sagged into the hold of his chains.

"Go right ahead," he said, managing to sound both disdainful and resigned. "Chew my throat out. I don't care. What else are you going to do to me anyway?"

A good question. I glanced at the other alphas as I

dressed. Marco's eyebrows were raised, his mouth slanted at a crooked angle. Frustration smoldered in West's eyes.

Nate let out a huff of breath and snapped at the rogue's neck. But he didn't let his teeth even graze the skin. He swung his massive form around, shifting back into a human.

"Take him away," he said to the guard with a jab of his hand. "I don't want him in my sight unless we need him again."

"What about the raccoon shifter he was talking about?" I said as the guard moved to drag the rogue out of the yard. Alice sprang to help him, since Nate was obviously too agitated to join in. "If someone here helped the rogues, shouldn't we—"

"It doesn't matter," West said flatly. "One of the guards who died was named Keith. Unless that's a particularly common name among the kin here, I'm going to assume the rogues made sure their 'ally' couldn't tell any tales."

"He got what he deserved, then," Nate rasped. He stalked back and forth across the yard as he tugged on his shirt. He'd destroyed his jeans in his hasty shift. If the situation hadn't been so tense, I might have enjoyed the view. "Traitor. Betraying his own people like that." He ended the sentence with an agonized growl. "One of *my* people."

Aaron turned to him. "Nate," my eagle shifter said.

Before he could continue, the other alpha shook his head with a jerk. "I need to think. We'll talk more in the morning. Give me the night to make some sense of this. If

I can." His gaze found me. "I'm sorry, Ren. This isn't at all how I'd have wanted your first night here to go."

"I know," I said softly. It killed me, seeing him in so much pain. "If you need anything from me..."

"For now I'm not going to be good company to anyone."

He swiveled on his feet and strode toward the estate house.

My bed felt too empty when I woke up in my room. I rolled over and stretched my arms across the soft mattress, feeling the vast space on either side of me. Just like at the avian estate, the dragon shifter's bed was sized for five. For me and my mates. But none of those mates had spent the night this time.

The breeze drifting through my half-open window was warm, but I shivered as I sat up. The rogue dog shifter's chuckle echoed in my head. *He let us right in, your precious kin did.*

What could have compelled one of the shifter kin to help an attack against their own kind? And if one could be persuaded, who was to say others hadn't been?

No wonder Nate and the others had been so upset. I was only just starting to understand the bonds between kin and their alphas, and even I was horrified.

Hopefully Nate had calmed down and cleared his head by now. I might not understand the situation completely, but I knew enough to realize we had to talk and come up with some sort of plan of action around this new revelation.

Also like the avian estate, my suite and those assigned to the alphas were down a separate hall from the rest of the house, with a branch that led to a private common room. This one had a view into a stand of redwoods. A long oak table stood at one end next to a sideboard laid out with breakfast foods. At the other, closer to the window, was a cluster of armchairs and couches.

The smells of fried eggs and sausages turned sour in my mouth at the sight of my gathered alphas.

Nate was bent over in one of the armchairs, his head in his large hands. Marco was lounging in another, ever the casual cat, but I could see the tension wound all through his sleekly muscled body. Aaron stood behind one of the couches, his hands braced on the top, as if he couldn't bear to sit down. Alice shadowed him, standing by the window. And West stopped his pacing between the sitting area and the dining table to scowl at me.

"You're here," he said. "We can finally talk."

I could have protested that no one had bothered to wake me up to tell me they needed me, but I wasn't in the mood to bicker with him.

"I'm here," I agreed, walking over to the sitting area. "Do we know anything new?"

Nate shook his head. He raked his fingers through his dark hair and straightened up without quite meeting my eyes. "I still can't believe it. My kin don't turn on each other. We agree to work together to each other's benefit, despite our differences. That's the whole *basis* of being disparate kin."

"Clearly it's not," Marco said. He might have been aiming for a teasing tone, but it fell flat. Nate glared at him.

As the bear shifter opened his mouth, Aaron cut him off. "It isn't just the disparate kin," he said, the rasp in his dry voice more pronounced than usual. "The owl shifter who attacked Ren at my estate was kin too."

My jaw went slack. "What? But she—"

She'd had no kin mark, I meant to say. Then the memory snapped into focus in my head. The avian woman who'd attacked me had been wearing gloves. I'd thought it was odd at first, and then I'd been so distracted by the attack and her story afterward that I hadn't thought to question it.

But Aaron had talked to her more, after we'd found out she'd been coerced into going along with the rogue group through the threats against her son. He was her alpha. Of course he'd have known.

Everyone's gaze had shot to the eagle shifter. "And why is this the first we're hearing about *that*?" Marco asked.

Aaron's hands flexed against the top of the couch. "I was hoping it was an isolated incident," he said thickly. "That the rogues had gotten lucky and manage to find one rare kin member they had the means to manipulate. Do you think I *wanted* to say my kin were untrustworthy? But now I have to think our kin aren't so difficult to manipulate after all."

My heart squeezed. The avian alpha had told me before that the other kin-groups often looked down on his people. Saw them as something lesser because of their forms. I wished he'd told me everything, but that attempt on my life *had* only happened yesterday. His reluctance made sense.

"It's not about kin being trustworthy or not," Alice jumped in, coming to stand beside him. "The rogues are still behind all of this. The rogues are still the ones we have to deal with."

"I don't know," West said with an edge in his voice. "When we stayed in *my* kin's village, the rogues didn't get any help from my people. So maybe we can make a few judgments about where to trust and where not to."

"This is the first time any of my kin has betrayed me in the sixteen years I've been alpha," Nate said, getting to his feet. He glared at the canine alpha. "And I never heard of it happening before my rule either. We'll see what happens on your estate, won't we? If we ever get there, and you canines don't throw the rest of us off to be anarchists or whatever you've got planned."

"I do what's best for my kin first," West snapped. "That's what pack loyalty is."

"Hey!" I broke in, raising my hands. I stepped between them, close enough to Nate to make him step back. I glowered at West. "We've got enough problems without you guys taking jabs at each other. From now on we have to be extra careful even among kin. Stay on guard. I don't think any of us should go off alone. It's mostly me they want to hurt, but they killed the alphas last time too. I want all of us safe. From the rogues, and from each other."

I shot Nate a look too. He dropped back into his

chair, his mouth twisting. "You're right. I'll watch my temper."

West looked faintly chagrined, which was about as good as I could hope from him. "All right. What other brilliant plans do you have to share with us, Sparks?"

Oh, great. Another chance for him to judge me and find me wanting. I groped for a reasonable answer. "The rogue we questioned said a bunch of his group is assembling in the south, didn't he? We need to find them and take them down before they can launch some new surprise attack on us."

"Great. That's the what. The tricky part is the how. Got anything on that front?"

"Wolf boy," Marco said from his chair. "Heel. Unless *you've* got some genius master plan, I don't think you should be knocking our Princess of Flames's contributions." He gave me a hesitant smile.

"Before anything else, we need to know where the rogues are," Aaron said, cutting off any snarky remarks West might have added. "This is partly my fault for not warning the rest of you sooner that our kin might be worthy of suspicion. I'll go. I can survey the area quickly in eagle form while drawing relatively little attention. I'll be able to spot their movements without getting close enough for them to know I'm anything other than your average bird."

The corner of his mouth crooked slightly upward. His guilt shone in his clear blue eyes. I swallowed hard. "You shouldn't go on your own either. I can come with you."

"As a dragon?" he said gently. "You can't let people

see you soaring around all over the place, Serenity. And you're still working on your endurance. It may take hours, even days, for me to locate them, if I do at all."

I frowned, but I couldn't argue with his logic. And even if neither of those points had been true, the rogues would scatter the second they saw a dragon swooping by. We needed them to think we weren't on to them so we could turn the tables on them. Create our own surprise to get the upper hand.

"*I* won't have either of those problems," Alice said. "You'll have some company."

Aaron turned to his sister. "I want you to stay here with Serenity. She needs protection more than I do."

"She's got these three lunkheads looking after her already," Alice protested, motioning to the other alphas. The insult didn't seem to bother Nate, but West's lip curled in distaste and Marco looked vaguely offended.

"Lunkheads who can't spend ten minutes together without arguing," Aaron said lightly. "I'm thinking she might want a break from the guys here and there. Please, Alice. I'm not planning on taking any unnecessary risks. I won't engage the rogues—not even if I see one alone. It's a simple reconnaissance mission."

"Can you at least come back for the night?" I put in. "Report back anything you've seen, even if it isn't much? You're going to have to sleep sometime anyway."

Aaron hesitated and then nodded. "That's fair. I'd rather not cause you more worry than I need to."

He came around the couch and walked up to me. When he touched my cheek, I raised my face instinctively to his. He kissed me fleetingly, but in the brief moment our lips met, all I wanted was to cling to him and refuse to let him go. His salty, ocean-breeze smell wafted over me, settling just some of my nerves.

"I'll see you tonight, Serenity," he said, looking me straight in the eyes. Hearing my full name in his measured voice still made my heart thump. It was only because he sounded so sure that I managed to let go of him.

Alice came up beside me as her brother headed out. She touched my shoulder. "I wanted to go with him because we'll be stronger together, not because I don't think he can handle himself. He'll deal with those rogues if he needs to."

"Yeah," I said. But what if the rogues in question had guns?

Aaron had promised he wouldn't engage them. If they never knew the eagle soaring overhead was a shifter, they wouldn't bother him, right?

I rubbed my temple. "Well, the rest of us can't just sit around waiting for him. What are we going to do in the meantime?"

"There's a welcome party already set up for tonight," Nate said quietly. "I didn't want to cancel it. We'll have to keep a close eye on who comes into the estate."

"All the more reason for me to stick to Serenity like glue," Alice said, sliding her hand around my elbow. Her grip was gentle but confident.

A chilling thought struck me. "It's the guards we'll be counting on to check who comes and goes, isn't it?" I said. "What if the raccoon shifter isn't the only one the rogues have gotten to?"

Nate's posture stiffened. "I chose the guards for this estate carefully. The people I knew I could count on."

"One of them already proved you wrong," West pointed out.

"If I find out any more of them..." Nate couldn't seem to finish the sentence. A frustrated rumble emanated from his chest.

"Why don't we at least talk to them?" I said. "I'm pretty sensitive to people's motivations. If we gather the rest of the guards together and I talk to each of them for a bit, then we know we don't have to worry about any more traitors."

Nate sighed. "You're right. I can call the ones who are off-duty in for a briefing, and you can talk to them during that. I'll get that round-up happening now."

He pushed to his feet and made for the door. As I moved to follow him, West exhaled with a mutter under his breath. "Well, this should be an interesting show."

I decided not to even dignify that comment with a glare.

CHAPTER 5

Ren

"Line up along the wall," Nate ordered the group of guards. This new set, a couple dozen shifters, shuffled to spread out through the massive dining hall.

I waited until they'd settled in against the exposed tan brick. They'd just come off duty after I'd spoken to the guards who'd now relieved them. So far I hadn't seen any reason for concern. As far as I could tell, Nate had chosen his guards pretty darn well.

The other alphas had wandered off on their own business, but Alice had stuck around. She was sitting perched on the edge of one of the big pine tables. The way her sharp eyes scanned the line-up made her look every bit the eagle even in human form.

"This is our dragon shifter, Serenity Drake," Nate said, pitching his voice to carry through the room. He stumbled slightly over my full name, so used to using the nickname I was most comfortable with. "On her first visit here, she wanted a chance to meet and speak with all of you. As your alpha, I know you'll do your kin proud."

We weren't telling them the full reason for this gathering, but I knew word had passed on about my talk with the rogue. They knew this was more than just a friendly chat.

"Hi," I said to the first guard in the line, dipping my head slightly so he could catch my scent. He did the same in return—a ferret. He looked it. His dark eyes studied me warily from his pointy face. But he was tough, too, his arms ropey with muscle. "Like Nate said, I'm Serenity, but I really prefer if you call me 'Ren.'"

"Mitchell," he said. "It's an honor to meet you, dragon shifter."

He didn't totally mean it. I could taste his hesitation. But that wasn't new. I'd gotten the same impression from about half of the other group too, as if they weren't quite sure their kin were better off or worse with me around.

"What made you volunteer to serve as a guard here?" I asked.

His gaze slid to Nate, and I sensed nothing but warm devotion from him then. "It is the *greatest* honor to be at my alpha's service. If I save my kin even a little trouble on his behalf, I couldn't ask for more."

I caught a thread of what he didn't say in the dip of his voice. He blamed the trouble they'd just had here on me. Well, fair enough. The rogues wouldn't have launched their assault if they hadn't known I was on my way to the estate. I'd gotten the same vibe from the other doubters.

Of course, some of Nate's kin still gave off those wafts

of dragon-shifter awe I was in the process of getting used to. A little farther down the line, a mountain goat shifter bobbed on her feet almost giddily as she bowed her head to me. Her eyes shone with excitement.

"I heard you got the truth out of that rogue with your dragon fire last night," she said after she'd answered my questions. "That he couldn't do a thing to stop you! It sure is a good thing having a dragon shifter around again."

"I'm glad you think so," I said with a smile. I just hoped I could live up to her expectations.

I'd spoken with about half of the guards when I reached a muskrat shifter who greeted me with a wide grin. It should have looked friendly, but there was something slightly twitchy about him that set my nerves humming.

I gave him the same greeting I had the others. His bow was a little jaunty. I'd have liked him if it wasn't for that aura of discomfort he was giving off.

"The name's Orion," he said. "Big name for a little guy. My mom had the idea it'd make me more impressive."

The corner of my mouth tugged into a smile despite myself. "You must be decently impressive if your alpha chose you for his guard."

"Ah, I do what I can. A little stealthy sneaking here, a little rat-jitsu there." He winked.

Again, I was struck by the sense that he wasn't anywhere near as at ease as the front he was putting on was meant to imply. He wanted me to laugh and move on. And the sooner I did, the happier he'd be. But the emotions roiling beneath his jaunty demeanor weren't annoyed or skeptical.

No, if anything he was *scared* of my attention. Hmm.

Well, I'd let him think he was getting what he wanted. "Keep up the good work, then," I said, and moved on.

None of the other guards rubbed me the wrong way. When I reached the end of the line, I could see several of them shuffling their feet, eager to be dismissed. They'd just finished a long shift on duty. With this scheme, I'd probably irritated all the ones who already weren't impressed by me.

I touched Nate's arm and leaned close to him. "They can all leave except Orion. I want to have a one-on-one chat with him."

Nate's eyes darkened. "You think he's in league with the rogues too?"

"I don't know yet," I said. "So don't go into full grizzly mode on him right away. There's just something off about him. Different from the ones who are just thinking I might be causing more problems than I'm solving."

Nate bristled. "If anyone says anything—" he started, and I patted his arm.

"It's fine. I don't blame them. Let's find out what's going on with the muskrat, all right?"

Subtlety might not have been Nate's strongest point, but he managed to single Orion out without being totally obvious about it. My bear shifter ambled over to the doorway before telling the guards they were dismissed. As they filed past him, stances relaxing, he caught the muskrat shifter and tugged him to the side.

"Just one more thing I wanted to go over with you," he said, as if it had nothing at all to do with me. A couple of the other guards looked over curiously. From across the room, I felt the tension clench through Orion's body.

No, he wasn't happy about this development at all.

Alice hopped off the table. "Should we go somewhere a little less... expansive? I feel better when I've got the walls closer at my back."

"Yes," Nate said. "I think a little privacy is in order for this talk."

"I... don't understand?" Orion said as Nate ushered him to a side door at the other end of the hall. "What's this about?" He carefully did not look at me.

"I think we'll figure that out once we've gotten to the talking part," Nate said. "Come on." He gave the muskrat shifter a light cuff to the head to nudge him onward. Maybe not that light, actually. The smaller guy winced.

Orion had done a good job playing the joker in the middle of the line, but as we tramped deeper into the palace, his nerves started to show. He raked his hand through his bristly black hair. His narrow jaw worked. When Nate opened a door down the hall and motioned him in, his legs balked for a second before he complied.

I followed, glancing around approvingly. Nate hadn't picked anything that resembled a chilly interrogation room. The room looked like a study: built-in bookcases stuffed with books and binders, a desk at one end and three leather chairs at the other. Alice, who seemed to enjoy a higher vantage point, hopped up to sit on the edge of the desk. The rest of us took the chairs.

Orion twisted his hands in his lap. His gaze darted to me and then settled back on his alpha.

"You have to know," he said in a strained voice, "I had no idea that attack was going to happen. I haven't done anything to threaten the security of the estate or my kin here. I *wouldn't*."

"I *thought* I knew that," Nate said in a low voice. "But after what happened the other night, I'm sure you can understand we need to be absolutely sure of all of you. If something is bothering you, you can tell us."

Orion's choice of words hadn't escaped me. He'd picked them very carefully. He hadn't known about the attack. He hadn't done anything to hurt his kin. That left a whole lot of other things he might have known or done —or that he might mean to.

"Orion," I said, as gently as I could manage, "you can obviously tell we singled you out for a reason. *Something* is eating at you. Something that wasn't a problem for any of the other guards. I don't know if you realized, but one of a dragon shifter's abilities is a sensitivity to people's emotions and motives. I know you're scared of me. I just want to know what it is you're afraid I'm going to do."

He wet his lips. "Isn't it normal to be a little nervous of someone who can transform into a mythical creature a gazillion times bigger than me?"

Damn it, he had me smiling again. "My dragon form isn't quite that enormous. And actually, from what I've seen, your reaction isn't normal. Most of your kin and the other kin I've talked to know that my job as dragon shifter is to look out for all of you. I'm on your side. An ally, not an enemy. Unless you've been doing something you know would make you *my* enemy."

The muskrat shifter looked at his hands. His fingernails had ragged edges, as if maybe he'd been nibbling on them. His mouth twisted. "I haven't done anything," he said.

"But maybe you've been thinking about it?" I suggested. "I've got to assume that if the rogues got to Keith, they've tried feeling out some of the other guards too. Maybe you've talked to them. Maybe you've considered doing more."

His shoulders tensed. He didn't need to say anything. I could read his guilt as clearly as if it was printed on his shirt.

It radiated off him strongly enough that Nate picked up on it too. He stood up, looming over his guard. His voice came out in a growl.

"If you've had any contact with the rogues at all—"

I held up my hand, and Nate swallowed the rest of his threat with a rumble.

"Just tell us," I said to Orion. "We'll figure out the truth one way or another. If you really are loyal to your kin and your alpha, then after what the rogues did here today, you should know that helping them at all is going against everything you're supposed to stand for."

"I just wanted to hear what they had to say," Orion blurted out. "Some of the things they said, it sounded as if they had ideas that would make things better for all of us kin, not just them."

He snapped his mouth shut as if he hadn't meant to say even that much. His fingers dug into the seat cushion.

"Okay," I said. "Fine. Like what? I want things to get better for all the kin too."

Orion shot me a frantic glance. I felt the emotion in that too. "No," I added, "I'm probably not going to like your answer. But I still want to hear it. I swear on my blood as dragon shifter that I'm not going to punish you just for sharing your thoughts. All right?"

The forcefulness of my oath seemed to convince him to speak. "I'm still deciding what I agree with," he said. "I had to meet you first, I had to see— They've been saying things like maybe we shouldn't be ruled by a shifter who doesn't have any ties to any of our kind. That—" His eyes twitched toward Nate. "That maybe our alphas should be focused completely on us and not on trying to make all the other groups happy."

"Doesn't have any *ties*?" Nate said, his voice rising. "The woman you're looking at is the daughter of the alpha who ruled our kin before me. Hell, Orion, we don't even *have* a kind other than not being one of the other main kinds of shifters. And you were ready to see blood spilled—"

"No!" Orion protested with a squeak. "I told you, I didn't know—I never wanted—"

"Now look," Nate said, grabbing him by the front of his shirt. Energy rippled over him as if he were about to shift. I jumped up too. This wasn't how I'd wanted this talk to go.

I pushed Nate back with a hand on his shoulder. His anger rolled over me, but his expression softened when he met my eyes.

"It's okay," I told him. "I asked for those answers. I

can handle it. Maybe you should wait outside for a few minutes? I think it might be better if I talked to Orion alone." Without an alpha's temper in the room with us.

Nate let go of Orion's shirt. The muskrat shifter cringed in his chair. Nate's hands closed into fists at his sides and opened again. "We can't trust him. I don't want to leave you alone with that traitor."

"He hasn't betrayed anyone yet," I pointed out. "And I can turn into a dragon, remember? I think I can handle one muskrat."

"I'd bet she can too," Alice put in. She strode over and motioned to Orion. "Stand up. I just need to make sure you haven't got any weapons on you."

He stood stiffly as she patted him down. She stepped back, setting her hands on her hips. "All clear. Come on, Mr. Grizzly. What's he going to do—batter her with books? We can wait right outside the door." She arched an eyebrow at me. "Scream if you need us."

Nate grumbled wordlessly, but followed her out. As the door shut with a thud behind them, Orion sank into his chair. I sat back down too. He peered at me with eyes that suddenly looked flat and hopeless.

"Are you going to fry me now?" he asked. "Like you did the rogue you caught?"

Ah. I guessed I knew what he was most scared of now.

I leaned forward. "I wasn't planning on it, but I will if I have to. It doesn't hurt—at least not much. Not enough to kill you." He didn't look all that comforted by those facts. Moving on... "I only used it because your rogue friend wouldn't talk to us at all. What matters the most to

49

me is protecting all the kin. I don't want one more person dying on my watch."

Orion rubbed his mouth. "He isn't my friend," he said. "I'd never associate with anyone who'd do what they did."

"But you're still not sure you want to turn your back on the rogues completely," I said, reading his body language. "You still think they might have a point. About me."

He sucked in a ragged breath. "We haven't had a dragon shifter since I was five years old. I only just met you half an hour ago. I don't know."

But he wanted to. I felt it underneath the uncertainty and the fear. He *wanted* me to convince him that he could believe in me. As much as he'd probably hoped the rogues would offer guidance he could believe in when he'd entertained their ideas.

I didn't know how to give him that. The best I could think of was to be honest.

"Can I tell you a secret, Orion?" I said.

His expression turned puzzled. "All right."

I dragged in a breath. My chest clenched before I forced it to release the words. "I've been worried about all the same things you have. Whether I can really help. Whether me being here is changing things for good or bad. And I'm still figuring that out. I didn't even know I was a dragon shifter a month ago. I didn't even know there was any such thing as shifters."

Orion stared at me as if he couldn't imagine not knowing. I guessed he probably couldn't. "But you're supposed to be leading all of us."

"Yeah," I said. "That's the sticking point, isn't it? But I can tell you this. I'm doing everything I can to learn and accept my role as quickly as possible. I know I *want* to be the dragon shifter you all need. I'll do whatever I can, whatever it takes, to see all of you happy and safe. And from everything I've seen, the rogues want the exact opposite of that. They'll be happy to tell you otherwise so they can use you, but look at how they treated your colleague. He helped them, and they killed him to protect themselves. Maybe you can't trust me yet, but you have to see you can't trust them."

He lowered his head. When he spoke, his voice was quiet. "So what do you want from me?"

Good question. I considered it. "I want to know anything you've found out about the rogues and their plans, so I can make sure what happened here yesterday doesn't happen again."

He nodded. "I can't tell you very much. They wouldn't tell me very much unless I proved I was allying with them. They approached us when we patrolled outside the estate walls, the times when we ended up on our own for a moment. I think they must have had people watching the area just for that—but maybe not anymore. The one I talked to was a fox shifter."

"How were you supposed to reach out to them if you decided to join their cause?"

"I'm not sure." He spread his hands. "They said they'd reach out to me. I don't know how."

"But if they did, you'd tell us now?"

He raised his head. "Yes," he said. "I'd come straight to my alpha."

I tasted the honesty in his words. He was still scared, still unsettled. But he was upset by what he'd seen the rogues do too. He truly hadn't done anything to hurt us yet.

Maybe to trust me, what he needed was for me to trust him.

CHAPTER 6

Nate

Orion's voice bounced off the close walls of the holding cell. "But I cooperated!" my former guard protested as one of my current guards jabbed him with a tranquilizer. "I answered her questions. I didn't do anything wrong!"

"You talked with shifters you know are out to screw us over," I replied, just barely holding my anger in check. "You didn't tell me what was going on. You considered going along with them. Be glad that our dragon shifter is merciful, because believe me, I'd like to do a lot worse to you than this."

The muskrat shifter opened his mouth as if to argue more, but the drug was already taking effect. His chin wobbled, and then his body sagged. The guard holding him let him drop onto the bench in the holding room. She turned to me. "Should I chain him?"

I shook my head. "If he comes to enough to shift,

those things won't hold him. Just make sure he's kept tranquilized enough until I decide where he'll end up next."

She gave me a sharp nod and threw one last disdainful look at her former colleague. With a sniff, she stalked out of the room. Our would-be-traitor wasn't going anywhere anytime soon.

I stalked down the hall, my muscles itching. I wanted so badly to shift. To shift and rage, clawing the floor, battering the walls, letting out every bit of the frustration that had been boiling up inside me since last night.

But I wasn't just an animal. I knew turning into a raging bear wasn't going to help anyone.

"Are you all right, sir?" the guard asked me.

"Yes," I said. "Go on back to your regular duty. And thank you."

No, I wasn't all right, not at all. I'd misjudged my own kin. I'd brought my new mate, the mate I'd been waiting for from the moment I became alpha years ago, into the worst kind of danger. I couldn't even promise her she'd be safe within my estate's walls.

She should have been looking forward to a grand celebration tonight, one that would have rivaled the reception she'd gotten at the avian estate. Instead we were limiting the guests, checking them over for weapons, setting an atmosphere of anxiety. And everyone would have been anxious anyway after the other night's attack. Word about that would be all over the countryside now.

We needed to shut those rogues down for good. Maybe we should have before we'd even found Ren.

It'd become easy to ignore the problem over the years.

In the aftermath of the previous alphas' murders, I'd been too busy learning my role to offer a counter-attack. Some of the old guard had tried to track down as many of the rogues as they could, but the perpetrators had gone into hiding. And they hadn't stirred up much trouble since then.

Because they thought they'd gotten what they wanted, I had to assume.

I prowled through the halls of my home, not entirely sure where I was going but needing to keep moving. I stopped when I spotted one of my attendants coming around a corner.

"Vernon," I said. "Is the avian alpha back yet? Aaron?"

The panda shifter blinked his big round eyes. "Not that I've heard, sir. I can ask in case I missed his arrival."

I waved that suggestion off. If the avian alpha had returned, I couldn't imagine he'd have been quiet with his news. "That's fine. Just come find me if you see him."

I stalked on, my feet carrying me without thinking to the wing that held my advisors' quarters. The place where the other night's attack had been the most brutal. My people had rushed to clean up as quickly as they could, but a bullet hole still marked one wall. There were scratches in the floorboards no buffing was going to erase.

My jaw clenched. I knocked on the first door at my right.

Yvonne opened it a moment later. The stately horse shifter had been one of the first of the former alpha's advisors to really take me under her wing when I'd been hardly more than a boy. Now, her silver hair was slicked back from her face in its usual braid, but her eyes looked wearier than usual. Heavy with grief.

"My alpha," she said with a dip of her head. "What brings you here?"

"I just wanted to check in on you. See how you're doing."

"Well, about the same. Do you want to come in?"

I accepted the invitation. Yvonne wouldn't have offered it if she'd wanted to be alone, even when it came to her alpha.

The sitting room at the front of her quarters smelled the same as it had since I was a boy, like clover and sunlight. The coffee table that had used to sit between the two low couches was gone, though. I realized with a lurch of my stomach why. It must have broken in the skirmish.

"If you wanted to change rooms, there are a couple of suites unoccupied," I said.

Yvonne shook her head. "We lived in these rooms for thirty years, and I'll remain until you no longer have any use for me as advisor."

"Well, that day is never going to come." I gave her a halting smile. It reassured me a little that she managed to return it. I groped for another topic of conversation. "What do you think of our dragon shifter?"

"Oh, she's a fiery one, isn't she?" Her smile grew, but it looked bittersweet. "Saying she'll put an end to the rogues. Is she really prepared for the battle ahead?"

As much as I valued Yvonne, my hackles rose at the question. "Ren has faced more troubles in the last few weeks than most of us have to deal with in a lifetime. I'd say she's handled herself well."

"There now." The horse shifter patted my arm. "I didn't mean anything by it. Of course you'll stand by your mate. I simply meant that it seems the pressure on her is only going to keep growing. She's had no training, no time to even ready her mind for what's ahead. I hope she can stay steady, but it would be hard for any of us."

"Exactly," I said. A little heat crept into my tone, remembering some of the standoffish reactions my guards had given Ren. "It isn't fair to her, being brought into our world when the community is in more chaos than it's ever been. But we'll figure it out, the five of us, together. It's what the rest of us trained for. No one should question that."

Yvonne looked up at me with her clear, sad eyes. "Sometimes I think we have human minds just so that we can question things. Even the people trying to show us the way."

Ren

"Your guests are starting to arrive," Alice announced. "Do you want to go check them out?"

I paused where I'd been wandering my sitting room, trying to think if there was anything I'd missed with Orion, some way I could have better won him over.

Some way to feel completely confident I'd won him over at all.

57

The view out the window told me the sun was still over the trees. "I thought the welcoming party was happening tonight."

Alice shrugged. "Apparently the disparate kin also have a disparate sense of time." Her lips curled up at the joke. "I just figured maybe you could use a distraction."

Yeah, I probably could. I sighed and rolled my shoulders, not sure meeting a bunch more strangers—stranger shifters who weren't half as impressed by me as the other kin-groups I'd met—was the kind of distraction I wanted. But it was the kind I had.

"I guess I'd better change into something a little fancier," I said, looking at the jeans and tee I'd pulled on this morning. I'd already checked out all the wardrobes in the dragon shifter suite. There'd been one with casual clothes, thank God, but most were full of the posh formal wear the regular kin apparently liked to see me and their alphas decked out in.

I'd had my eye on one dress already: an ankle-length satin gown in an indigo shade so deep it was almost black. This didn't seem like the right time for anything flashy. I pawed through the hangers for it and chucked off my clothes to put it on.

"Any news from Aaron?" I asked his sister as I adjusted the fall of the fabric. Even if Nate's kin didn't totally buy into me as leader of the shifters yet, they'd have to admit I at least looked the part.

Alice grimaced. "Nothing so far. But he's got a few hours left before I'll be ready to bite his head off. He should have let me go too. Not that I mind hanging out with you, but from what I've seen you can handle yourself around here just fine."

"Hey, I agree with you," I said. "I guess *two* golden eagles soaring around together might have looked a little conspicuous, though."

Alice grinned. "Not half as conspicuous as if he'd had a dragon keeping pace with him."

"Okay, okay, that was a dumb idea. I fully admit it. But I have a much better one now." I sniffed the air. "Someone's roasting chicken. Really, really tasty chicken. What do you say we go find some of that?"

"I'm in."

My heart started thumping a little faster as we headed toward the house's main doors. I wanted to peek outside before I walked right out, just to see what I was getting into, but that didn't seem leaderly at all. Squaring my shoulders, I pushed open the door and strode down to the courtyard as if nothing about the people down there could faze me.

Alice had been right. Several dozen shifters were already gathered on the clay tiles of the courtyard, most of them ones I didn't think I'd seen in the estate earlier. And all their heads turned toward me as I came down the steps. Quite a few faces brightened up. That made up for the ones that only looked thoughtful.

The atmosphere didn't feel all that celebratory, I had to say. I guessed it was hard to really party when four deaths and several injuries hung over the estate.

"Hi," I said, going up to a small cluster of bear shifters who appeared to be happy to see me. "I'm Ren. Um, I think this whole get-together is for you to meet me, so... here I am!"

One of the women touched my arm. Her hand trembled a little. "You've been through a lot to make it here," she said. "I'm glad we could make it here to greet you properly."

The guy beside her leaned close as if to share a secret. "People are saying you have more fire than the dragons before. A different kind."

"That's true," I started to say. Another of the women laughed with pleasure.

"We can burn all those rogues back to the darkness where they belong," she crowed.

Okay, that was a more violent turn than I really wanted this conversation to take. "I'll deal with them as well as I can," I said, and swiveled to look for someone else to introduce myself to.

By the time Alice and I made it to the refreshments table, I'd endured a multitude of questions about my special fire-breathing, more skeptical looks than I could count, and a few outright glowers. At least I had lots of practice with those thanks to West. I didn't feel all that hungry anymore, but I grabbed a glass of wine.

Where were my alphas anyway? Nate probably had more estate business to tend to, and Aaron was off on his reconnaissance mission, but the other two should be around somewhere.

It didn't really matter. I just wanted an excuse to take a breather. I meandered off around the side of the house with Alice in tow.

The gardens on the disparate estate were mostly

prickly hedges dotted with flowers interspersed with even pricklier cacti. The vegetation was pretty in its own right, with a pungent perfume, but I was careful not to touch any of it.

"Not the friendliest flowers, are they?" Alice remarked, jabbing the chicken leg she'd grabbed toward one cactus.

"At least people know better than to mess with them," I said.

Voices carried across the grounds from up ahead. I slowed, my ears perking.

A wall of the same adobe bricks that made up the house stretched partway into the gardens. The voices were coming from beyond its arched doorway. I crept over and peeked inside.

The doorway led into a smaller courtyard with a gazebo surrounded by a moat of burbling water. Marco was leaning against one of the marble posts by the moat, a glass dangling from his hand, his eyelids lowered in a typical languid expression. A few other shifters—ones I recognized from Nate's guard—stood in a semi-circle around him. Their postures were full of bravado.

"Is that all you've got to say for yourself, cat?" one of the guards said. "Look at you. You still think you're better than us, don't you?"

"I have total respect for all kin," Marco said mildly. "Excluding those who align themselves with the rogues, of course."

One of the others took a step closer to him. "Your kind always turns your nose up at us. We've seen it. But the dragon shifter has turned her nose up at you, hasn't she? Picked our alpha to confirm as her mate without a second glance at you."

I bristled at the jab, both that she'd made it at all and at the thought of how Marco might respond. When his own people had hassled him about his status with me, he'd put them off with a bunch of blustering about how easily he was going to work his charms on me and finish the "job."

I almost stepped through the doorway to put an end to the confrontation before I had to hear anything like that again. But Marco's calm voice stopped me.

"Serenity makes her choices as she sees fit. I'm not so arrogant to think I know better than a dragon." He gave his harassers a thin smile.

"Aw, look at the kitty cat," the first guy said. "Completely pussy-whipped and not even fully mated yet."

Marco chuckled. "I'd rather be whipped by her than left with whatever dregs you court."

The guy's face flushed red. "Now listen, you—"

"Hey," the guard next to him said. "We've hassled him enough. Our alpha will be checking in soon. Let's leave this one to 'enjoy' his solitude."

The first guy let out a huff, but the three of them rambled off in the other direction. Marco rolled his eyes at their retreating backs.

He didn't even look upset. He'd taken all those comments in stride, even though they must have stung his pride. Instead he'd just sounded proud of *me*.

I swallowed hard, turning back to face Alice. "Give

me a few minutes? I'll be with one of my alphas, so I should be safe."

"Sure," Alice said. "If you need me later, just give me a shout."

She drifted back toward the party, and I slipped through the doorway. Marco straightened up when he saw me. His eyes, their indigo irises almost the same color as my dress, glittered as he took me in.

"Aren't you a sight?" he said with a crooked grin. "Shouldn't you be out hobnobbing with your adoring public?"

I made a dismissive sound. "They're not all that adoring. Which is fine. The adoring ones are exhausting too. I'm just pacing myself."

"A wise decision." He held my gaze with that hint of hesitation I'd felt from him before. "Is there anything you needed from me, Princess of Flames?"

"Can we... talk?" I said.

His grin softened. "I think that could be arranged. Look, we've got this handy gazebo right here."

He offered his hand and led me up the steps. When he sat on one of the benches inside, I took the spot next to him. His presence didn't set me on edge the same way it had a couple days ago. We still had a lot of ground to cover, and he obviously knew that. But he was trying to make up for the mistakes he'd made. Even when he didn't have any idea I'd know how he was behaving.

And when I wasn't on edge, it was impossible to ignore the warmth of his body beside me. The bond drawing me even closer. I curled my fingers around the edge of the bench.

"I wanted to ask... The things you said, that I overheard—the way you talked about me— You said you've had to learn not to show any weaknesses around your kin. What has it been like since you've been alpha? Before I came into the picture, I mean."

Marco inhaled sharply. "Princess, you don't need to hear about that. And I'm not going to insult you by trying to justify what I said."

His hand was still cupped over mine. I turned mine over to intertwine my fingers with his and squeezed. "I'm asking because I want to know. You're not justifying. You're just letting me in on things I wasn't there to see."

"Well." He was silent for a moment. "You know the sort of temperament cats have. It carries on to cat shifters. We've always had issues with authority. So being alpha requires a certain attitude... of detachment, and confidence. You have to put on a show. I think I've gotten fairly good at that, and I've still faced over a dozen challenges since I came of age. It'd have been a lot more if I'd had a weaker disposition."

"Oh." I said. That had been how many years? Five? And he'd had to fight to hold onto his position more than twelve times already. "That seems like a lot already." My gaze went to the scar that notched his eyebrow. I raised my other hand to trace the pale line. "Is one of those fights how you got this?"

"The only one I almost lost." His mouth tightened, but he shrugged. "Dealing with challenges wasn't fun. But it's the way it is. I've gotten into the habit of turning on that cocky attitude when faced with any criticism. That's not an excuse for insulting you, though."

I glanced up at him. "No. But the fact that I haven't fully taken you as my mate... That makes your kin question you. They can't even have kids until we're together." My stomach twinged with a pinch of guilt. None of the shifters could produce children until their alpha was fully mated. The longer I delayed with Marco and West, the longer their people stayed barren. "I could understand if you were upset that I hadn't been willing to consummate with you yet."

Marco blinked at me with what looked like honest surprise. "What? No." His voice dropped. "I mean, I very much look forward to that time coming... assuming it does. But I've always known I'll have to be worthy of that bond. And clearly I haven't been yet."

"But when it could make such a difference—"

"*No*," he said firmly. He turned more toward me, letting go of my hand to touch my cheek as he held my gaze. "Ren, do you know what I've been realizing the past two days? Feeling this distance from you, watching you come into your own... If I could give the damned alpha position to someone else and just have you, I'd take that deal in a heartbeat. I've never wanted the authority as much as I want to earn my place at your side. I wish I could give you more than just words to prove it."

My heart was pounding, but not with nervousness now. I felt his fingers against my cheek through every inch of my body. The warmth of them loosened my tongue.

"You could show me," I said. "Show me how much you want me."

Lust flared in his eyes. "Princess," he murmured, with

so much longing it set my skin on fire. He bent his head and pressed his lips to mine.

The kiss started out slow and gentle. His mouth was sweet against mine, the spicy smell of him surrounding me. It wasn't halfway enough to satisfy me. I gripped the front of his dress shirt and pulled him closer.

With a groan, he kissed me harder. My lips parted, welcoming, and his tongue swept in to tease me. His free hand slid up the side of my dress. His thumb stroked in soft circles closer and closer to my sheathed breasts as one kiss bled into another.

It felt so good. So fucking good the rush of pleasure started to carry me away. The careening sensation made my breath catch. I hadn't intended to—did I really want to—

Marco pushed away from me with a rough gasp. He kept his hands on me, one at the crook of my jaw now, the other beside my breast, as he gazed into my eyes.

"You're not ready," he said. "Not really. It'll take more for me to show I deserve you in every possible way. But I will. I promise you I will."

My hand was still caught in his shirt. I dropped it. "Marco, I—"

"It's all right, princess." He kissed me again, just a brush of his lips against mine. "I'm not going to beg. I'm certainly not going to blame you. When I've earned my place, when you're sure of me, you can come to me."

CHAPTER 7

Ren

SO WHAT ARE *you waiting for exactly?* Kylie's latest text said. *Just grab those hunks and have your way with them already!*

I shook my head with a smile she couldn't see. I sure wished it felt as easy as she made it sound. *I've been making progress. I've got two official mates now.*

Woohoo! Now we're talking. Was the second one Nate or Marco? Or did you manage to thaw out the chilly wolf?

I outright laughed at that, flopping back on my bed. The chilly wolf. Yeah, that was an appropriate description for West. Other than the rare occasions when he suddenly turned scorching.

Nate, I replied. *Things are still a little tense with the other two.* Although less so with Marco after this afternoon's conversation. It wasn't enough to completely make up for the callous way he'd talked about me, but it got us partway there. I wasn't sure I'd be able to completely trust him—and my body's reactions to him—until I'd seen how he acted when we were among his kin.

And how was it? Don't kiss and tell doesn't apply to besties, you know that.

Not in Kylie's book, anyway. But there was only so much I was willing to commit to written record.

It was good. Really good. I think I'm getting the hang of this mate thing.

Oh, my little Ren, all grown up.

I wrinkled my nose at the phone, but the comment was fair. I hadn't gone all the way with any guys in the entire time I'd known Kylie before now. Even when I hadn't known I was a dragon shifter, something inside me had felt that bond to my destined mates. Something that had gotten out its claws anytime I got too hot and heavy with a guy.

But that was fine. I'd take even West over any of the boys and men I'd met before now.

A knock sounded on the door. Nate's rich baritone carried through. "Ready to go, Ren?"

"Pretty much," I called back, shoving myself upright. "You can come in." *It's party time,* I wrote to Kylie. *More later.*

I met Nate in the sitting room. It was hard not to stare at his impressive form packed into that formal suit. I was still wearing the same gown from this afternoon. After a brief escape from the growing crowd, I felt ready to face the official celebration. Everything before this had just been a warm-up.

Desire kindled in Nate's gaze as he took me in. He wrapped a brawny arm around my shoulders to pull me close to him. I closed my eyes and leaned into his kiss. He felt more relaxed now. Less rage simmering beneath the gentle exterior. But I knew if anyone ever threatened me again, the grizzly would be back in an instant.

"Orion is locked away and on the tranquilizer," he told me when he pulled back. "The guards have been carefully monitoring everyone else who's arrived. I don't think you need to worry."

"I know you're taking every step you can," I told him. My stomach twisted. "Is it really necessary to lock Orion away? I mean, he hadn't done anything really wrong *yet*. Maybe he never would have."

"He tried to lie to us," Nate said. "He let the rogues' ideas get into his head. We can't trust him. And I'm not wasting one of the guards I *can* trust following his every move."

"Fair enough," I said. But it still didn't sit right with me, treating someone like a criminal for just thinking about taking the wrong path. Not much I could do about it right now, though. "And has Aaron turned up?"

Nate shook his head with a frown. "His idea of 'night' might be different from mine. I'm expecting him to show up soon."

The twist in my stomach tightened. "If something happened to him—"

"Hey." Nate tipped my face toward his and kissed my forehead. "You don't need to worry about that either. I don't know where he is, but I know if he were really hurt, *you'd* know it. You're his mate. That connection will take time to grow, but if anything were really wrong, you'd feel it."

Great. I could assume Aaron wasn't on the verge of death, but there were so many ways his expedition could have gone just somewhat wrong.

I bit back my frustration and took Nate's hand. "I guess we'd better get out there."

Dinner was being served in the courtyard—a much less formal affair than the banquet at Aaron's estate. I sat with Nate at a table at the head of the yard, Marco at my other side and West beside him. The empty chair where Aaron should have been sitting niggled at me. Alice caught my gaze from the other side of it and frowned in sympathy.

As attendants brought us plates of food, the other revelers moved from serving table to serving table. They stacked their own plates and then started eating standing up or sitting on the benches scattered around the fringes of the yard.

There were at least twice as many people as when I'd been out here before, but the atmosphere still felt subdued. The music playing had a slightly mournful sound to it even though the melody should have been lively. I guessed we all had too much on our minds.

While we ate, the other shifters also drifted past our table to make their greetings. A lot of them smiled more brightly at Nate than at me. Well, they'd known him a hell of a lot longer.

One elderly badger leaned his chubby hands on the edge of the table and fixed me with a beady stare. "Word is you've got special powers beyond compare," he said. "Going to sort out all those rogues right quick, are you?"

Maybe I'd been a little hasty making that speech at the funeral yesterday. "I'm going to do my best," I said.

"We won't have any peace here until that poison is rooted out and destroyed," he said with a firm nod.

The "poison" the entire rest of the shifter community had failed to destroy for the last sixteen years? Yeah, no pressure there.

The next group, a gaggle of lady voles, squealed over me and asked me to do a little shift for them to see. I brought my talons out of my fingers, and they cheered. I was feeling more welcome after they moved on—at least until a sharp-faced bear shifter ambled over.

"I hear one of our kin is in a prison cell right now," she said, glancing from me to Nate and back again, as if she figured the offense had to be my fault. "What's that about? We're locking each other away now?"

Nate cleared his throat. His voice came out low and firm. "We've always used the holding rooms under the estate to deal with kin who break our laws, Mildred. You know that."

She sniffed. "And what law has this one broken?"

Nate glowered at her. "That's not a matter for public discussion."

"It seems like a lot has changed since we had a dragon back in town."

My back stiffened as she flounced away from us. "Ignore her," Nate muttered. "She's always been a difficult one."

It was true that most of his kin were friendly to me. I spent another hour, at the table and then circulating through the crowd, smiling and laughing at jokes and telling a few of the less traumatic stories from my life among humans. But even when the shifters were smiling back, I wasn't sure how much to believe in their warmth. Did they really trust me, or were they just better at hiding their uneasiness than some of the others?

Alice came up beside me. "Time for another breather?"

"Yeah," I said with relief. "What did you have in mind?"

"It seems to me there's no reason we shouldn't help restock the wine table," she said with a grin.

We meandered into the estate house and down to the wine cellar. And a massive wine cellar it was. I didn't think I'd seen so many bottles in my life, even in a liquor store. I stopped and stared at them.

"I don't know where to start."

"Ah, we can always just hang out here for a bit and then let the attendants pick. That's their job anyway." She propped herself against a crate and cocked her head at me. "I'm guessing the life you had before my brother and the other alphas found you was pretty different from this, huh?"

"Uh, yeah, that would be the understatement of the year."

"Tell me about it. I've always wondered what it's like on the human side of things."

I let out my breath. Where to start? "Well, I'm not sure my 'human' life was all that normal. When my mom was still around, we always lived pretty simply. Her first concern was making sure we didn't draw attention to ourselves. And then after she left... I ended up having to leave the apartment and live on the streets. I didn't have a real home for more than five years. Let alone a home like this." I waved to indicate the entire estate.

"That must have been rough," Alice said, her tone going serious. "You don't let it show, when you're out there talking to the kin."

I shrugged. "That's not the side of me they want to see, right? The side that's human. Weak."

Alice grimaced. "I wouldn't call surviving the lowest rungs of the human world with no support and no powers *weak*, not by a long shot. You know, I can't say I've had to experience anything like that, but I have needed to spend a lot of time keeping up a strong front. It wears you out. The more you can be your real self, the easier it'll be on you in the long run."

"I guess that makes sense." I looked down at my hands. "It's just hard to know what anyone expects. There's still so much I have to get used to."

"This place is a bit of a change from the avian estate, isn't it? The different kin-groups have their own attitudes. Or attitude problems." She gave me half a smile. "We avians usually get along best with the canine crew. We both believe in strong bonds and keeping a united front. The felines and the disparate community, it's a bit more of a free-for-all. Everyone for themselves."

Okay, so maybe it wasn't that Nate's kin resented me for the attack. Maybe this was just the way they always were. That possibility was weirdly reassuring.

"Everyone wants so many different things," I said. "It's kind of... overwhelming. I don't know how I'm going to make them all happy."

Alice knuckled my arm. "Probably you won't. But I guess the best you can do is listen to everyone, and your alphas, and don't forget what's in here too." She tapped her head. "And you find whatever balance seems to be the best fit. See, simple! I have all the answers."

I had to laugh. "Right. I guess I'm all set then."

Her gaze drifted toward the door, and I abruptly realized that the flexing of her muscles wasn't just her usual bodyguard-like readiness. She was feeling edgy too. I didn't need any special senses to figure out why.

"You're worried about Aaron," I said.

She rubbed her mouth. "He's a big boy. He can take care of himself. As he likes to remind me on the regular. But... I thought from what he said that he'd be back by now."

If even Alice was worried enough to admit it, my anxiety wasn't just me being over cautious. I hesitated. Why shouldn't I change her orders? Technically I had at least as much authority over the shifter kin as Aaron did.

"You know what?" I said. "We've waited long enough. I want you to go looking for him. And if he has a problem with that when you find him, you can tell him to take it up with me."

Alice blinked at me. "Really?"

"Absolutely. That's a direct command from your dragon shifter."

Her mouth stretched into a real grin. "Now I'm *really* glad we've got you back."

We grabbed a couple bottles of wine somewhat at random so it'd look like we'd done more than just disappear. But when we emerged into the courtyard, it occurred to me that there were other orders given that I didn't totally agree with. I wasn't going to go against Nate's authority—but I could try to temper his harshness with a gesture of my own.

I picked up a new plate and snatched a little of this and a little of that off the tables. The kin watching were probably speculating about a dragon shifter's appetite. Let them wonder.

I carried the plate into the house and down the stairs into a different part of the basement. The part where we'd confronted the rogue just yesterday. I caught sight of Orion through the second window I glanced into.

The former guard was hunched over on his bench, his head in his hands. My heart wrenched.

The guard on duty walked over. "Dragon shifter," he said with a respectful bow. "What do you need?"

I held up the plate. "I'd like to bring this in to him."

The guard paused. "I wasn't told—"

I fixed him with a firm stare. "I'm your alpha's mate and dragon shifter. All I want to do is bring the prisoner a little dinner. He's too drugged up to shift, isn't he? He doesn't look like he's going to be any threat."

"Yes. Yes, he should be subdued. My apologies."

The guard pulled out a key and unlocked the door. I stepped inside tentatively.

Orion raised his head. The muskrat shifter's eyes were glazed. A dribble of drool shone at the corner of his mouth. He was at least aware enough to notice it and swipe it away when the back of his hand when he saw me.

"Dragon shifter," he said in a dazed voice. "What are you doing here?"

"Bringing you some food from the celebration out there, since you're not allowed to get it for yourself."

I offered him the plate. He stared at the spread of food for a few seconds before he reached for it. Then he just set the plate in his lap. He gazed at the meal for a moment longer and then peered up at me, squinting.

"Why would you bring me this? What does it matter to you what I eat? I'm a traitor."

I crouched down so my eyes were level with his where he sat on the bench. "I don't think you are," I said. "I don't think you'd decided one way or the other yet. And I think that matters. I know how hard it is to figure out the right thing to do when you're being pulled in different directions. What you choose in the end, that's who you are."

He wet his lips. His fingers clutched the edges of the plate. "Thank you," he said hoarsely. I couldn't tell if he meant the meal or the sentiment. Maybe both.

My heart felt a little lighter as I headed back to the party. So naturally I had to run into West right then.

He paused in the hall as I stepped out of the stairwell. His eyes narrowed. "What were you doing down by the holding cells?"

"Trying to make sure we don't turn another kin into our enemy," I said. "Is that all right with you?"

He held my gaze for a moment. Then he sighed and turned away. "I just hope you know what you're doing, Sparks."

So did I. He had no idea how much I did.

CHAPTER 8

Ren

I watched the last of the guests drift out of the courtyard, and a weight settled in my gut.

It was just past midnight. The attendants were clearing the tables. The courtyard was quiet. No one was left except the shifters who lived on the estate.

And Aaron still hadn't returned. Alice hadn't either. She wouldn't have known exactly where to look for him, so I guessed her absence shouldn't be surprising. But he'd said he'd be back for the night. He couldn't have denied that it was absolutely, one hundred percent nighttime now.

Nate came up behind me, touching the small of my back. "Let's go inside," he said. "If he turns up, we'll hear about it."

I nodded, but my feet dragged as we headed back to our section of the estate house. Marco and West caught up with us.

"Nightcap, anyone?" Marco said. "If we're all going to fret about eagle boy, we might as well enjoy ourselves at the same time."

We made our way down the narrow hall to our private common room. West stalked across to the far windows as Marco went to the liquor cabinet to mix the drinks. Nate sank down onto one of the couches. I paced from one end of the room to the other and back again as if I could outrun my anxiety. So far the motion was only making me feel more tense.

Marco handed me a shot glass. I tossed it back in one gulp. The alcohol burned down my throat and spread warmth through my chest. But it only took a slight edge off my worries. Several more might have done the trick, but I didn't think drinking myself into a stupor was a wise idea.

"You should try to get some sleep, Ren," Nate said. "We all should. If something has gone wrong, we'll need all our strength."

I rubbed my arms. "I don't think I *can* sleep." I was too wound up. Wondering about all the things that could have happened to Aaron that wouldn't trigger our mate-bond. He could be captured by the rogues. Too injured to fly home but not quite badly enough for the pain to tug at me.

I wanted him *here*, plain and simple. Someday I was going to have to get used to being apart from my mates, but I didn't think it was supposed to happen this soon after we'd consummated. It didn't feel right. This was the first night any of them had been this far away, and the distance gnawed at me.

"Come here," Nate said gently. He patted the couch cushion next to him.

I bit my lip, but I went to him. As I dropped down next to my bear shifter, he reached for my shoulders. His strong thumbs rubbed in steady circles over the tensed muscles there. They dug in, and the tension started to release.

"Okay, that's good," I said, my eyelids drooping. "Keep on doing that."

I heard his smile in his inhale. He eased his hands farther down my mostly bare back, kneading the muscles along my shoulder blades and spine. With each press, the tightness melted a little more.

And as it melted, a different sensation started to tingle through my body. His hands against my bare skin sparked a heat I should have expected, considering those hands belonged to one of my mates.

The heat shot straight to my core. My panties dampened. Oh, there were a hell of a lot of other parts of me I'd like those hands on.

My rising desire must have scented the air. Nate paused with his hands just below the base of my neck. He leaned closer, his breath spilling hot over my skin. "Maybe there's a little more I could do to distract you? Let out some of that tension?"

My body ached with longing. Fuck, yes. With all the turmoil since we'd arrived, I'd barely had time to feel anything good. But it seemed like far too long since I'd lost myself in the bond between me and my mate.

My *mates*. My eyelids fluttered open. I leaned back

into Nate's touch instinctively, encouragingly, but at the same time my gaze sought out the other alphas.

Marco set down his empty glass, his eyes intent on me and Nate. A gleam of lust danced in them. West had turned, his stance tensed, but I could feel the hunger radiating off him.

Nate slid his hands around to cup my breasts. A gasp slipped out of me as he teased his fingers over the peaks, my nipples pebbling. Marco licked his lips. He moved as if to step toward us and then seemed to catch himself.

Waiting for me to give him the go-ahead.

I wanted all of them. All of them there with me, being with me in every way, taking my mind off the one who wasn't here for at least a little while. If even one more of them left my side—

The thought made my throat close up. I set my hands over Nate's to still them. The hot flush of desire coursed beneath my skin. I stood, pulling him with me.

"I think we should take this to my bed," I said, my fingers twined with Nate's. My gaze locked with Marco's and then West's to make it clear that my "we" included all of us.

A brilliant smile spread across Marco's face. "There's nothing I'd like better than to serve you however it pleases you," he said in a heated tone.

West wavered on his feet, looking torn. I held my other hand out to him. "I won't ask for anything you can't walk away from. I just want you all with me. How much is up to you."

I heard him swallow. Then he stepped toward us. "All right," he said, even more gruff than usual.

We slipped down the hall to my chambers. When we reached the end of my bed, I turned to face my mates. With a yank, I unzipped my dress. It crumpled into a heap at my feet, leaving me all but naked.

The heat in the room must have risen by ten degrees. I shivered with it, giddy—but suddenly uncertain. I'd been with Aaron and Nate at the same time before, but three guys... I needed them, but I wasn't exactly sure how.

"Just tell us what you want, Ren," Nate said, his voice slightly ragged. "We're right here with you."

I looked at each of them, my breath catching. "Shirts off. Pants too." Might as well spread the nakedness around a little.

Marco smirked as his hands darted to unbutton his shirt. West stripped down more hesitantly. A faint glow emanated from around the bandage he wore just below his left shoulder. A fae magic wound, I was pretty sure, though he'd avoided talking with me about it. In the midst of my rising lust, I made a mental note to be careful of it. Mess with that and he might never touch *me* again.

Nate discarded his clothes with a few jerks and the snap of a button. He was ready to get started, clearly. He stepped closer to me, his chest brushing mine, and claimed my mouth.

I moaned against his lips, reveling in the force of his kiss. He gripped my waist. A third hand grazed over my back to undo the clasp of my bra, a hot presence at my left side. Nate released my mouth to swipe his tongue across the crook of my jaw. I tipped my head to the side to give him full access to my neck, and Marco was right there to meet me.

As my bear shifter nibbled his way across all the sensitive spots on my throat, my jaguar shifter caught my mouth with his. He stroked his hand over my breast, tweaking the nipple until I whimpered.

Nate dipped his head to lave my other nipple into an even stiffer peak. Marco trailed his lips across my cheek to nip my earlobe. I shivered with pleasure, awash with sensation. Every part of my body was tingling.

But my mouth was being neglected again. I gasped as Nate's hand dipped between my legs, and my gaze flew up to find West's.

My wolf shifter was standing a few feet away, his hunger blatant on his face and coiled all through his stance. I met his dark green eyes. Nate's thumb stroked over my clit. I let out a whimper and mumbled, almost a plea, "West."

His jaw twitched. His eyes flashed. "Fuck," he said, and then he was striding toward me. He gripped my head as Marco brought his mouth to my collarbone. My heart skipped, ready for West to devour me. But as his fingers curled into my hair, he first pressed the softest of kisses to my forehead. The bridge of my nose. My cheek. My lips parted, wanting, waiting. The path he was tracing was the sweetest torture.

He finally brought his mouth to mine just as Nate tugged my panties down and slipped his fingers between my folds. Marco swiped his tongue around my nipple. I moaned into West's mouth, and the tender control he'd been keeping snapped.

His kiss ravished me, his tongue sweeping in to tangle with mine, his teeth grazing my lips. I kissed him back just as hard, wanting to plunder and be plundered. Marco was suckling my breast and Nate was kissing his way down my belly and oh, God, if I literally exploded from all this bliss, which seemed like a real possibility, I hoped the cleaning staff wouldn't hate me too much.

Nate eased me back on the bed. He knelt between my legs. I sucked in a breath as he swirled his tongue over my clit. Then Marco was kissing me again, his spicy coffee smell filling my senses. West licked one breast and fondled the other. Every nerve in my body was humming with fulfilled desire.

But I had even more desires that needed fulfilling. Nate pumped his fingers in time with the movements of his mouth, and I cried out at the jolt of pleasure. My whole body felt like a harp string being plucked harder and faster to reach a crescendo. When I shattered with it, I wanted to bring my mates with me.

I eased my mouth away from Marco's, panting. "Nate, inside me, please."

He didn't need more than my mumbled request to understand. His mouth left me for a few aching seconds before the hard length of his cock replaced it, tracing over my core from my clit to my opening.

I moaned hungrily and arched my hips. Nate gripped them, holding them off the bed and sliding into me with a groan of his own. The feel of him filling me sent an eager shudder through me.

"My Princess of Flames," Marco murmured beside me. "You really are on fire."

"Mmm," was all I managed to answer. I wanted to set him on fire too. I ran my hand down his chest to the cock jutting from between his legs, slimmer than Nate's and almost elegant. Marco practically purred as my fingers curled around it.

I tugged him gently forward. The heat in his eyes turned blazing as he caught on. He eased himself down on the bed so I could bring his cock to my mouth. It twitched as I licked the tip.

Nate thrust into me, sending a fresh wave of pleasure through me. I rode on it right down Marco's shaft, curling my tongue around his silky hardness, tasting the salty musk of his arousal.

"Fuck, princess, I'm not going to last long like that," Marco said around a groan. Good. Let him come apart right here with me.

My other hand had fisted in the duvet. As my body rocked with Nate's thrusts and the pump of my mouth over Marco, my knuckles brushed smooth skin over lean muscle.

I hadn't forgotten my other alpha. West was testing the edge of his teeth against my nipple now. With an instinct that must have come with being a dragon shifter, being meant for moments like this, I reached down and knew exactly where to close my hand around his cock.

West's breath stuttered against my breast. "Ren," he rasped. I stilled my fingers, sucking Marco down again, tipping my hips to meet Nate's next plunge into me. Ecstasy flooded me from every direction, but I wasn't going to take what West wasn't ready to give.

The wolf shifter lay there rigid for a moment. Then

with a groan he pushed himself closer to me, welcoming my touch.

I slid my hand up and down his shaft in time with my mouth on Marco's, in time with Nate's inside me. A sense of bliss continued swelling not just from between my legs but my lips and fingers as well. From all of us together in this circle of pleasure.

Marco broke first. "Princess," he cried with a rough jerk of his hips. He moved as if to pull back from me, but I closed my lips around him tight.

His release spurted against the back of my mouth. I sucked it all in until he sagged beside me. He withdrew, kissed me on the lips for one long, aching moment, and then eased his hand down my body.

His lithe fingers found that bundle of nerves just above the spot where Nate and I were joined. They circled my clit, and the wave crested inside me. I gasped, squeezing West's cock. With a grunt he muffled in my hair, he spilled over. I followed, stars sparking behind my eyes, my whole body shaking with the force of my orgasm. As I clenched around Nate, he made a strangled sound and joined us in release.

We were probably quite the sight, the four of us sprawled together on the bed, limp and sated. But as Nate gathered me up and nestled into the pillows with me, the other guys joining us on either side, being with all of them felt like the most natural thing in the world. The best thing in the world.

Aaron's absence still gnawed at me, but it was a more distant pain now. Snuggling among my mates, I managed to drift off to sleep.

CHAPTER 9

Marco

THERE REALLY WAS nothing like waking up next to my mate. Her sweet smell laced the air, and the taste of her skin still lingered on my lips. Her body lay close enough to mine that its warmth traveled to me under the sheet.

My Princess of Flames was cuddled up next to Nate, who was lying opposite her. The glossy dark brown waves of her hair spilled over the brawny arm she was using as a pillow. Her head was tucked against the bear shifter's broad chest.

Some distant part of my brain suggested that I should feel jealous, but the only emotion rising through me was a swell of affection.

She looked content. Peaceful. It had been days since she'd been able to really relax, and she needed it after all the challenges she'd tackled—and tackled so well. Thinking back on how she'd faced down the fae monarch still gave me a flush of pride. Our dragon shifter was coming into her own by leaps and bounds. I'd already admired her when she'd stood up to me, confused but defiant, before she'd even known what she was. Now... She was magnificent.

So I couldn't resent Nate for giving her this comfort, even if my heart and the threads of the bond inside me throbbed with the longing for her to be just as much mine.

Really, it was pretty hard to resent anything at all with the memory of her mouth around my cock still fresh in my mind.

A couple days ago, I hadn't been sure when I'd even get to kiss her again. Me and *my* mouth—my stupid, stupid mouth. But last night we'd moved together like we were meant to bring each other pleasure. Maybe we were building a sort of peace between us now.

With a grunt, our other companion in the bed sat up. West raked a hand through his hair and shot a disgruntled look Nate's way. "Last time I sleep next to the bear shifter," he grumbled. But as he pushed himself off the bed, I didn't miss the way his gaze paused on Ren with a flare of desire.

Wolf boy's self-denial was reaching ridiculous levels. He could blame it on the mate bond and try to put up all the walls he wanted, but it was obvious every other part of him wanted her too. Ah, well. As long as he was denying himself, our dragon shifter had more attention for the rest of us.

As West grabbed his clothes and stalked out of the room, I eased a little closer to Ren. A joint cuddle didn't seem out of bounds. I pressed a kiss to the back of her neck and wrapped my arm around her waist.

Ren made a pleased sounding murmur and rested her arm over mine, squeezing my hand. "'Morning," she mumbled, her eyes still closed.

I traced my thumb in a slow circle over her soft skin. The feel of her against me combined with last night's memories had already gotten me hard. And that made me more daring. "Should we make it a particularly good one?" I asked.

"Mmm. You could try."

Well, that was a challenge I wasn't going to turn down. I trailed my hand up from her belly to the curve of her breasts. As I traced my fingers across the undersides of those soft peaks, she started to squirm. Her firm ass brushed my hard-on. I had to grit my teeth to clamp back a groan. But fuck, being with her like this was the most enjoyable torture I'd ever experienced.

I teased my fingers up, up the pert curves, and then flicked my thumb over one already hardened nipple. Ren gasped, her eyes popping open. I stilled my hand. She'd been half asleep. The last thing I wanted to do was overstep and lose what little trust I'd regained.

"Too much?" I said against her shoulder.

"Not enough," she muttered back. "Don't you dare stop."

I chuckled with a wash of relief—and hunger. As I caressed her breast again, I nibbled along the slant of her shoulder to her neck. Ren sighed, arching back her head.

The bear shifter stirred at the movement. An eager sound thrummed from his chest. He dipped his head to kiss Ren on the mouth. His free hand swept over her hip and thigh to the mound between her legs.

Ren whimpered, rocking into his touch. I flicked my tongue along the crook of her jaw and drew out another gasp. Dear God, there wasn't any joy in the world that could rival the sound and taste of our dragon shifter's desire. I could live on it and nothing else for days.

I was about to ease her onto her back so I could attend to her breasts with both my mouth and my hands when the door to her chambers thumped open.

"Stop messing around and get out of bed," West snapped. "Aaron's back."

～

Ren

I walked into Aaron's suite with bedhead and a dress I'd picked up off the floor, but seeing my missing mate ASAP was a hell of a lot more important than prettying myself up. The other three alphas strode in behind me.

Aaron was sitting on the edge of his bed. The weariness on his face and in the set of his shoulders made my heart squeeze. I went straight to him, cupping his face with my hands. He gave me an exhausted smile and hugged me to him.

My fingers slid into his golden hair. I bent down to catch his lips with mine, needing that contact. As if his kiss were the only thing that could convince me he was really here, back where he belonged.

"I'm sorry," he said when I eased back. His voice was

weary too, its rasp thickened. "I meant to be back sooner. I know how worried you must have been."

"It's all right," I said. "I'm just glad you're back now. And okay. What happened?"

"He got himself stuck," Alice said, her dry tone more solemn than usual. She was leaning against the wall across from the bed, her arms crossed over her chest, looking equally exhausted.

Aaron chuckled faintly. "That's a fairly accurate description. I spotted some shifter movement below just before I would have planned to head back. They've set up a little camp, a few trailers and tents... I dipped down to confirm they were rogues, heard them talking, and found a perch I could listen from. But I stayed too long. Before I had a chance to leave, a couple of avian rogues shifted and took their posts around the camp, one of them close enough to me that he'd have noticed me leaving and raised the alarm."

"Couldn't out fly a couple of lesser birdies?" Marco said, mildly teasing.

"There was a falcon there, and a vulture," Aaron said. "They could have done some damage. But I was more concerned that what I'd learned wouldn't do us any good if they knew I'd overheard it. They'd have changed their plans."

"So he just waited there until I turned up and distracted them," Alice put in. "You're lucky we've got our sibling bond, or Lord knows how long you'd have been waiting there."

Aaron rolled his shoulders. "You can believe I'm glad you got there as soon as you did." He raised his head to meet my eyes again. "Thank you for sending her. It was the right call."

"Remember that the next time you want to go off alone," I said. "So what *did* you learn? What were they talking about? How close are they? Do we have to start preparing?"

He raised his hand to slow me down. When I went quiet, he tugged my wrist to sit me on the bed next to him. I wrapped my arm around his, watching his face as he started to speak.

"It sounded as though we should be fine as long as we're here," he said. "Unless, I suppose, we stay longer than they're expecting. They're settled in about a three-hour eagle-flight from here. The plans I heard, they were talking about waiting until we were on the move again. It was clear they assumed that within the next few days we'll be leaving here and heading toward the feline estate."

"That is what would make the most sense," Nate said.

Aaron nodded. "They want to catch us along the way. Make an attack with the advantage of surprise, on terrain they feel will skew the odds even more in their favor." He glanced at me to add an explanation. "Normally we'd make it a road trip so we could stop and meet with a few of the more distant communities along the way. We save the jets for emergencies."

"We could make an exception in a case like this, couldn't we?" I said.

"But then we'd lose our chance of confronting them. As soon as we reach Marco's estate, they'll have to make different plans. They'll move into a new position."

"Well, where's this prime terrain they're hoping to catch us at?" West asked.

"I don't know," Aaron admitted. "Either they'd already decided and didn't see the need to mention it to each other, or they haven't decided yet and are waiting to see what actions we take first. I couldn't tell from the way they talked about it."

Marco brushed his hands together. "Well, it doesn't matter, does it? Now we know where they are. We'll go deal with them before they can set up their little surprise."

"I agree," Aaron said. "But the difficulty is how. They're monitoring the area around the estate. They'll know if we set off straight toward their camp and scatter before we get anywhere near them. I counted around forty of them there. From what the rogue prisoner said, that might be as much as half of their remaining number. If we strike, it needs to be in a way that ensures none of them escapes. Otherwise we'll just have to deal with them again later."

"I've definitely had enough of that," West muttered. "Enough with the constant fleeing and regrouping. As long as enough rogues are out there to stir up trouble, none of our kin are truly safe."

"*Ren* won't be safe," Nate said. He moved to stand beside me, putting his hand on my shoulder. "They've gotten away with too much already. It's about time they faced some consequences."

"An excellent sentiment," Marco said. "It still doesn't answer the question of how."

Aaron rubbed his mouth. He looked so tired I wanted to tell the others to leave, to let him rest, but I knew from the determination in his stance that he wanted this settled. He'd waited out the rogues and spent the rest of the night flying back just so we could have this discussion. So we could come up with a plan of our own. I didn't think he'd be willing to rest until he knew the information he'd brought back could be put to real use.

"We do have some advantage now," Nate said. "We know they'll be trying to spring something on us."

"The trek from here to Florida is pretty long," Marco said. "We can't be on full alert constantly. I'd like a way to completely turn the tables on them."

An idea tickled its way into my head. I straightened up next to Aaron. "You know what? I think we already have the answer right here."

CHAPTER 10

Ren

"I DON'T KNOW ABOUT THIS," Nate said as we tramped down the stairs toward the basement holding cells.

"We don't have a whole lot of options," I pointed out. "What are you going to do otherwise—leave him locked up and drugged for the rest of his life? How is he ever going to prove whose side he's on if he never gets the chance?"

"I'd rather he was proving it in a way that didn't potentially risk your life," my bear shifter muttered.

"We can protect ourselves, can't we? We'll have our own sentries. We can withdraw if we need to." I stopped at the foot of the stairs and turned to face him. "Do you actually think it's a bad plan, or are you just worrying about me?"

He frowned. "It's the best plan any of us came up with. I won't pretend it isn't. But you can't blame me for worrying."

I patted his chest affectionately. "All right, I won't. Just try to go easy on him. We want him to feel he can trust *us*, remember."

Outside Orion's door, Nate produced a key ring from his pocket. The guard on duty hung back as we stepped inside.

Orion jerked up at the movement of the door. He'd been sprawled on his back on the bench, his head lolling. The tranquilizer still glazed his eyes and dulled his reflexes. He swayed before managing to completely sit up. His gaze stayed on Nate, wary even though his narrow face stayed slack.

I could just imagine how his last conversation with his alpha had gone. But I didn't want any grizzly behavior in here today.

I grabbed a stool from the hall and sat down across from the former guard. Nate loomed behind me, as if to give everything I said the extra weight of his authority. We'd decided it was probably better if I did the talking. Mainly because he wasn't sure he could keep his temper.

"Orion," I said, and the muskrat shifter's eyes dropped to meet mine. "We might have a job for you. A way for you to redeem yourself with your alpha and your kin—to show where your loyalties really lie."

Despite the vagueness of his expression, a spark of hope lit deep in his gaze. "What is it?" he asked. "What do you want me to do?"

"You've talked to the rogues before," I said.

He nodded. "One of them."

"So if we sent you out to talk to them, there should be someone in the local group who'd know who you are?"

"Yeah." His eyes darted between me and Nate. "But I don't know where they are. I told you."

"That's all right," I said with a crooked smile. "*We* know where they are. You could just... happen to stumble into them after we pointed you in the right direction."

He focused back on me, his head tipping slightly to the left. A furrow had formed in his brow. "And then what would I do?"

"Well, if you're up for it... We'd pick a spot for you to lead them to. We'll have a story for you to give them, something like that we're going to be sneaking out of the estate and heading down a specific stretch of road, somewhere that looks good for an ambush. You'll pretend you decided to side with them and you're bringing this inside information to prove your worth. And then we'll be the ones to ambush them."

Orion was quiet for a long moment, just looking at me. "You want me to trick them."

"They're planning another attack on us right now," I said. "They've already killed how many kin over the years? They support the people who killed the last alphas —my fathers. My sisters, who were only seven and nine years old. If any of them surrender, I promise you I'll treat them fairly. But if they're going to insist on fighting us, we can either fight back or lay down and die. And I wouldn't ask anyone to do the second. Including you. That's why I wanted you to have this chance."

"Your dragon shifter is being incredibly generous," Nate put in, his voice just shy of a growl. "As am I as your alpha, letting her bring you the proposition in the first place. Are you going to stay with us or fight against us?"

I shot him a look, and he grimaced but shut his mouth. "Or stay here," I added, turning back to the muskrat shifter. "If you don't want to take the risk, I'd understand. Maybe there'll be another opportunity for you to show your loyalties. This is what we've got right now."

Orion sucked in a breath. "I—I could do it. I think it could work. I can't promise anything, but I—" He stopped and rubbed his forehead. His jaw worked. "I can't think straight right now. But I know that I regret not coming to you as soon as they approached me, alpha. And, Serenity..."

"Ren," I corrected him.

He looked up again, his eyes gone watery. "Thank you," he said. "For thinking of me. For trying to do right by all of us."

"Will you try too?" I asked gently.

"Yes," he said. "For my kin. For my alpha. And for you."

My throat tightened at the emotion in his voice. "Then I should be thanking you." I stood up. "We'll have to let the tranquilizer wear off," I said to Nate. "He can make a final decision then, when his mind isn't so fuzzy. I want him to go understanding exactly what he's agreed to."

Nate didn't look enthusiastic about it, but it wasn't as if we could send his former guard off to consort with the rogues in his current state anyway. When we'd shut the door, he turned to the guard on duty.

"No more shots," he said. "Let him come out of the daze. Keep a close eye on him. If he shifts or does anything suspicious, restrain him if you need to and call for me. When he's had time to totally recover, call for me then."

"Yes, sir," the guard replied.

"You have your dragon's sensitivity," Nate said to me as we headed back to the main floor. "Do you think Orion actually wants to help, or is he just looking for any way to get out of that holding room?"

I thought of the former guard's watery eyes and the wave of feeling that had coursed off of him at the end. "He really does regret what happened. He wants to be part of the kin again. I can't tell how well his nerve will stand up once he's out there with the rogues, of course."

"I guess there'd be no telling that with anyone." Nate sighed. "Well, we'll see how he feels to you when he's totally awake."

"How long will it take for the tranquilizer to wear off?"

"A few hours at least." He paused when we reached the top of the stairs. "So we have a little time. There's something I wanted to show you here. It might actually be a little familiar."

I perked up, my uncertainties about our plan momentarily pushed aside by a spark of curiosity. "What do you mean?"

He smiled. "You'll see."

Nate led me through a few hallways and up a broad staircase to the second floor. He opened a door to a large room in what was obviously one corner of the house. The first thing that caught my eyes was the sunlight streaming through two pairs of windows on the south and east walls.

I stepped inside, and my breath stopped in my throat.

It wasn't just that the room was beautiful, although it was. The walls around the door were painted in reds and golds and glossy greens: stylized animals frolicking through a forest here, an ocean there, and up here by the ceiling puffs of dancing clouds. The designs stretched all the way to the windows, where trees and waves curled around the frames. The floorboards beneath my feet were polished to a shine so soft I almost felt as if I were walking on silk carpet.

I walked into the middle of the room and turned around. A warm, sandy smell hung in the air, like the kind of rock perfect for sunning yourself on during a hot summer day... if you happened to be a dragon. Like the actual rock that lay on the floor beneath the windows. A few chairs with plump cushions and wooden arms scattered the rest of the space.

Yes, it was beautiful. And also deeply familiar. Tears had sprung into my eyes.

"When I imagined bringing you to my home for the first time, I pictured the visit being a little more relaxing," Nate said. "But at least before we go you can spend some time in here. It was your mother's favorite room in the estate." He took in my expression. "You remember it."

"Yes." I sank onto the stone slab. The sun-drenched warmth of its solid surface spread up through my hands. "She would bring me and my sisters in here when we complained about being bored. Sometimes my father—

my bear shifter father—would come with us. What did she call it?"

"The inspiration room," Nate said with a smile. "The first time I met her, she called for me to meet her in here."

"Even though I couldn't shift yet, I loved lying on this rock." I eased myself down on my side, soaking up the stone's heat and the beams streaming through the windows. "Sometimes she'd curl up around me here. All four of us would squeeze in together, or five if Da was there..."

I swallowed hard. Nate's expression softened. "You don't talk about them very much—your fathers and your sisters. You can, you know. I mean, if it's too hard, you don't have to. But if you want to talk to someone who remembers... I trained with your bear shifter father for four years before the attack took him. I didn't know you or your sisters well, but I remember watching you playing in the courtyard when you were visiting."

Watching us and wondering which of us would become his mate? And now here I was. The only one of my entire family left.

I swiped at my eyes and pushed myself back into a sitting position. "It is hard. Not just because it hurts, but also because... The memories don't come easily. I don't think there's any magic suppressing them now, but when it's been so long since I've practiced remembering them— I don't know where to start unless I see or feel something that triggers them."

Like that embarrassing breakdown when we'd first arrived. My face still heated at that memory.

But this place provoked better ones. I found, with an

ache in my throat, that I did want to share them. To make them more real by conjuring those dead and gone.

I pointed to one wall. "My oldest sister, Temperance —she used to make up stories about all the animals. One time she spent hours connecting every piece of the painting into one epic tale. I never knew where she'd go with it when she started. The story came out totally different every time."

My gaze fell on the chairs. "And my other sister— Mom always said she must have accidentally birthed a monkey when Verity came out. Verity couldn't sit still for more than a few minutes. In here she'd climb up on the chairs and make a game of leaping between them, seeing how long she could provoke her dragon wings out for."

"And Da..." I could picture him in my mind's eye. Big and brawny like Nate, but longer in the face and even darker haired. My chest clenched up. "I always wanted to see more from the windows. He'd sweep me up in his arms and hold me right by the top, and tell me about all the things we could spot from here to the horizon."

I felt the giddiness that had run through my little girl's body. The joy of having my father's attention focused all on me.

What would he, and my other dads, have thought of me if they could see me now? What would my life have been like if the rogues had never sent it brutally off course?

Nate ambled over and sat down beside me. I leaned against his shoulder. He took my hand, rubbing his thumb over the back. "You lost a lot," he said. "More than any of us can understand. We each lost one mentor. Your whole family is gone. I have no idea what that's like. But whenever you want to talk about it, you can come to me. To any of us. I think I can speak for the other alphas there."

"Thank you." Now that I had talked about my family, my heart felt a little lighter. "I actually think I'd like to spend a little time in here on my own before we go. If that's okay."

"Of course," Nate said. "I should take care of a few things around the estate before we move on. If you need me, one of the attendants will know where to find me."

He tipped my face toward his and kissed me softly. When he moved away my body was humming. I could feel his presence through our bond even after he'd left and shut the door behind him. While he was on the estate and that close to me, I didn't think I'd need anyone's help to find him.

I lay back down on the sunning stone and just drifted in and out of memories for a while. Weirdly, letting those fragments of my past rise up didn't increase the pain of my loss. If anything, they soothed it. It was a heck of a lot better remembering the happy times. Why should my only clear recollections of my family be my fathers' and sisters' last moments of panic and torment?

When I sat up again, my nerves felt more settled. I touched the edge of my phone in my pocket. I did have another kind of family that I wasn't going to leave behind completely. I'd promised Kylie I'd keep checking in. The last thing I wanted was her figuring I'd ditched her.

Hey, Ky, I texted to her. *Exciting times here. We're going to take the battle to the rogues. I came up with a brilliant plan... Well, we'll see how brilliant it is when we try it.*

Her response came a minute later. *Oh please. If you came up with it, of course it'll work. I can just imagine your dragon self smashing all those assholes.*

There was something pretty satisfying about that image. *I wish you were here to really see it. I guess we'll be near New York again before too long. We're heading to Marco's estate next, in Florida, and then West's is up in the Northeast somewhere.*

Oooh, Florida sun and fun! Where's his pad?

I smiled. *Apparently not far from Miami.*

That figures. He totally looks like the clubbing type. Make sure you keep him in line, you hear?

Before I could answer, someone knocked on the door. "Come in," I said.

An attendant peeked inside. "Dragon shifter," he said. "Nate requests your presence by the holding rooms."

Shit. It was already time to see just how brilliant my plan was. I sucked in a breath. Add another one to the many conversations with my bestie I was going to have to put off finishing.

"All right," I said. "I'm coming."

CHAPTER 11

Ren

It felt strange, being the only one of the shifters around me still in human form. I set my feet down as quietly as I could, moving with the others up the wooded hillside we'd chosen for our ambush. A loamy smell filled my nose. Furred bodies wove through the trees around me.

My mates and Nate's kin who'd joined us had all shifted as soon as we'd left behind the vehicles, stashed off the road. It made sense, since in their animal bodies they could move faster and more stealthily, extend their senses farther, and just generally be more badass. Nate and Marco padded along on either side of me, West loping along ahead of us. Aaron soared overhead alongside Alice, watching for worrisome activity below.

I could have been a hell of a lot more badass as a dragon, but the one thing I wouldn't be was stealthy. Not to mention it wouldn't do us much good if I burned out my limited shifting energy tramping through the woods and then had to do the actual fighting as a human.

Orion should have reached the rogues' camp last night. The plan was for him to tell them that we'd be passing along this stretch of road this morning—that we'd planned to slip away during the wee hours to avoid notice. They'd think they were coming right down to the road to ambush us there. But they'd run right into *our* ambush before they had a chance to see they'd been misled.

At least, that was how it was supposed to go. Assuming Orion came through and didn't just throw in his lot with the rogues. He'd seemed determined to follow my plan when I'd talked to him before he left, but also a little browbeaten. Maybe once he'd gotten farther away from my and his alpha's authority, he'd decided to take his chances with people who hadn't locked him up and drugged him. Even if they were murderers.

I really hoped I'd been right about him, though.

West slowed at the top of the hill. He walked to the crest where the ground slanted down again and glanced back at us. This was where we'd planned to stop.

Aaron dove from the sky, leaving his sister on sentry duty. He shifted as he reached the ground and made a graceful landing on both human feet.

"There's movement a few miles off," he said. "I'd guess they'll be here in half an hour or so. We should spread out downwind so they don't catch our scent before we're ready to spring."

I nodded. The other animals drifted back into the trees. I followed, staying by Nate's side. I was going to have to hang farther back than the others, because my smell wouldn't blend into the natural landscape as well.

There might be a few downsides to being the rarest type of shifter around. But I did mean to use my unique skills to my best advantage.

When Nate stopped, with a dip of his head toward me, I ran my fingers into his thick grizzly fur and pressed my face to his shoulder. He nuzzled me back.

Back on the estate, while we'd been making our final plans, Nate had tried to convince me I should sit the battle out. He'd made it through about half a sentence before I'd laughed and given him my best dragon stare. There'd been no arguments after that.

The kin who'd died had been my kin too. And I wasn't going to stand by while the rogues who'd destroyed their lives and my family's were still walking free.

I turned and reached for the tree we'd stopped beside. The best thing about being a dragon was flying. And I'd be damned if I was going to spend any time at all on the ground as soon as I could shift.

I scrambled up the trunk and clambered from branch to branch until I reached the ones too narrow to easily support my weight. Sitting with my back against the trunk, I scanned the forest. I wasn't quite high enough to see over the canopy, but I had a decent view between the branches around me.

There was Marco's black jaguar form crouching a few trees to our left. West's wolf had blended completely into the brush. Aaron made one last swoop through the sky and came to perch on an oak to my right.

A half an hour. We'd burned through at least ten minutes fanning out around the ambush point, I thought. It shouldn't be that much longer. But it felt like an eternity between every beat of my heart.

A branch cracked, and my pulse leapt, but it was only a sparrow flitting away. Damn regular animals. I resisted the urge to shuffle my feet impatiently against the branch.

Orion knew exactly where we were going to be waiting. He was supposed to lead the rogues right over this hill. If he was keeping his end of the bargain. If not... Alice was still keeping watch. She'd notice if the rogues looked like they were spreading out to try to take us by surprise instead.

The breeze changed course, and new smells filled my nose. Animal smells—and not the familiar ones of the shifters I'd arrived with—mingling with notes of aggression and anticipation.

The rogues were almost here.

I leaned forward on the branch, bracing my hands and feet against the bark. We didn't want to spring the trap too soon. Let them barge right into the middle of our ring.

Bodies rustled through the underbrush. Faintly, covertly, but in the quiet my sharp ears could pick up the sounds. My muscles tensed.

A small furry form scurried into view below. A muskrat, leading the supposed charge. Our Orion. I sent a silent thank you down to him, and then several more animals emerged between the trees.

Below my perch, Nate let out a grizzly bellow. We all launched ourselves at the rogues.

I ran along the branch and vaulted out into open space. My scales rippled over my body with the rush of the air around me. My wings whipped out, catching that wind. I stretched and snapped my jaws with my emerging fangs, and hurtled down into the fray.

The forest floor was a mess of writhing bodies. A black bear I knew was Thomas was wrestling with a puma. A scarred silver wolf faced off against Marco's jaguar. Aaron clawed at a huge weasel that tried to smack him out of the sky. And more, all around—a blur of fur and teeth and splashes of blood.

I let a dragon's roar rip from my throat. The rogues startled, giving my kin their openings. The puma whirled to make a run for it, and I dove, smacking it into a tree trunk with one taloned paw. A coyote stumbled backward and shifted into human form. He made a grab for the gun he'd been carrying wrapped around his narrow waist.

The echoes of long ago shots fired in my family home rang in my ears. Anger flared through me. Oh, no, he didn't.

I sucked in a breath and spewed out flame—the hot, searing, destructive kind. The coyote shifter yelped. Then he was nothing more than a charred body with a melted lump of metal in his hands.

There'd be others who were carrying weapons they'd meant to bring to their own assault. I swung around, scanning the fray. I had to pick any rogue off who'd come armed. They could hurt us too quickly. My alphas and my kin were too honorable to break their law about using man-made weapons, even when their enemies didn't care to play fair.

The click of a safety disengaging made my gut lurch. I swiveled and blasted the figure standing amid the trees before I had time to register anything more than her blond hair and the pistol in her hand. A guy who'd sprung into human form nearby fumbled with his own handgun. Before he could aim it, I turned him into charcoal too.

My muscles tingled as I swooped in the other direction. Another human form moved between the foliage at the other end of the clearing— No, wait, that was Orion. I guessed he figured he could defend himself better with size on his side instead of his muskrat teeth and claws. Naked, his hands clenched into fists, he punched a rogue fox shifter that came at him in the muzzle and then leapt out of the way of its snapping teeth.

I slashed my talons downward to knock the fox shifter to the side. As I dropped down to pin her to the ground, another human figure ran at Orion. A human figure clutching a gleaming dagger.

A rasp of protest broke from my throat. Orion spun around, but not quickly enough. The rogue slammed the dagger into his gut, all the way to the hilt.

Orion's lips parted. His body sagged. Blood gushed down from the wound.

No. Panic spiked through my veins, sharp and cold. I swiped at the guy with the knife, ripping the dagger from his hand and the skin from his arm. But in my distress, I lost my hold on my shift. My dragon's body crumpled back into my human one.

I stumbled toward Orion. He'd sunk onto his knees and was reeling backward. I caught his shoulders just before his head smacked the ground.

"Hey," I said. "Hey. Stay with me." Shifters could heal from a lot. I'd had my chest gouged by a rogue wolf and survived. If the dagger hadn't been that well aimed— if I could stop the bleeding—

Reddish flecks were already dappling the former guard's lips. Shit, shit, shit. I clamped my hand around the hilt of the dagger, suppressing the flow of blood there, as if that surface wound was really the problem and not the cuts he'd taken on the inside.

Orion shivered and groaned. "Dragon shifter," he murmured.

"That's me," I said brilliantly. "I'm right here. You did good. You did your kin and your alpha proud. You're a fucking hero, you hear that. So you'd better live long enough to celebrate that with us."

He gave me a sickly smile. "I'm doing my best. But I don't think—" He coughed and gasped at the wrench of the blade with the movement of his chest.

"*No,*" I said, with all the authority I could summon. "As your dragon shifter, I forbid you from dying right now."

He tried to chuckle, but it came out more like a gurgle. Oh, God, there really wasn't anything I could do, was there?

"There's something... didn't tell you..." His voice was fading.

"It's okay," I said. "Just—just rest."

"No. You need... There's a feline kin. Someone... someone high up in the families. Calling the shots. Allied... with the rogues. They listen to him. The rest of the group—every rogue remaining... Ready to attack all together. You have to..."

His throat worked, and his body spasmed. "Orion!" I cried out, but his eyes had already fogged. "No, no, damn it."

I could feel it, as much as I wanted to resist what my senses were telling me. He was gone.

I sat back on my heels, my shoulders slumped. Then I flinched around at a thud behind me.

West had just tackled the fox shifter. From their positions, she'd been about to leap at me. His wolf was twice as big as her form. She squirmed and clawed, but she didn't stand a chance.

And she clearly knew that too. Like so many of the rogues before, she wasn't letting herself be taken prisoner. West shifted one of his paws to get a better hold on her, and she rammed her neck into his claws.

He jerked back, but it was already too late. He'd severed her throat. With a snarl of disappointment, he sprang off her sagging body.

West looked around at the dwindling fray and shifted into human form. His gaze caught mine. He jerked his chin toward Orion.

"He's passed?"

I swallowed hard. "It was just—the cut was too deep —it happened so fast. I tried everything I could think of."

My hands, tacky with the muskrat shifter's blood, clenched in my lap.

West's eyes dropped to them and rose back to my face. A shadow passed through his expression, from dark to light. "Yeah," he said quietly. "You did." He paused. "Ren—"

"We've got a prisoner!" someone shouted. A panting Thomas hunched over a sinewy body he'd managed to hold in place by the wrists. Alice had pinned the guy's ankles with her talons, still in eagle form.

"And I've got another," Marco announced, sauntering from amid the trees with a bobcat he held by the scruff of its neck and its restrained hind legs. His fingers tensed as the rogue struggled to break free. Nate shifted and moved to help him.

I pushed myself onto my feet. Too quickly. My legs wobbled, my stomach feeling as if I'd left it behind down by the ground.

West caught me by the shoulders. "Hey," he said, his voice somehow rough and gentle at the same time. He pulled me into a hug, tucking my head under his chin. We were both naked, but with the image of Orion's dead body lingering in my head, his blood staining my hands, there was nothing sensual about the embrace. I leaned into the heat of West's body seeking only comfort, from the mate I'd never expected to offer it.

He stroked his hand over my hair, and my hands slipped against his chest. Shit, I was getting blood all over him. I jerked back, not knowing where to put them. West looked down at himself, the smears of blood over the lean muscles, and shook his head.

"It's okay," he said. And then, in more the tone I'd have expected from him. "I expect you'll make plenty more messes than that before you're done, Sparks."

As I made a face at him, Aaron came up beside me. He offered me a strip of moss to wipe my hands. "I think we'll need your help questioning the captives," he said. "They don't seem any more inclined to talk than the other rogues have been."

Of course. I dragged in a breath and took in the results of our ambush. At least a couple dozen bodies littered the forest floor—all of them, as far as I could tell, rogues, other than Orion. A couple of Nate's other people were sprawled, having their wounds tended to by their kin, but none of the rest of us had taken a fatal injury. There'd been more rogues in the attack party than I could see around me, though.

"Some of the others got away?" I said.

Nate nodded. "A few cowards ran when they saw the way the battle was going and moved too fast for any of us to catch them. But only a few."

Damn. I looked at the bobcat and then the rogue pinned on the ground. "You've got a choice. You can talk to us now or you can talk in my fire."

The man on the ground glared at me. The bobcat hissed. Well, I guess that answered that.

"Pour down the flames, and we'll toss them in," Marco suggested. "I don't think they'll be going anywhere once you're got them in the hot spot."

"All right." I glanced at him. "Orion told me there's an important feline shifter, one of your kin, who's been calling at least some of the shots. Making plans with the rogues."

Marco's eyes darkened. "Interesting," he said, an edge creeping into his voice. "Let's see what these two have to say about that, shall we?"

I closed my eyes, reaching back to my sense of my dragon self. The change came over me more slowly this time, lengthening and expanding, nerves twitching. I'd already exhausted a lot of my energy during the fight. But I had enough to make this interrogation count.

I loomed over the others in the middle of the small grove. My kin moved to clear a space. I focused on the burn tingling at the base of my dragon throat. On my anger at Orion's death and the other deaths the rogues had caused. On my need to know what else they might have in store for us.

Then I opened my jaws and let the violet flames stream down.

Marco threw the bobcat into the fire first. It shuddered and expanded into a woman's form, huddled in the midst of the flames. "Who among my kin have you been talking to?" Marco snapped immediately.

"I haven't spoken to anyone," the bobcat shifter said in a whimper. "No one tells me anything. I just did my best to help."

"Are you aware of any allies among the feline kin—or any other kin—that the other rogues have been talking to?" Aaron asked, phrasing his question carefully.

She shook her head. "No one except the one on the disparate kin's estate. And that one." She pointed toward Orion. "Much good as he did us."

"What were you going to do if your plan to ambush us here didn't work?" Nate said.

"I'm not sure."

West cleared his throat. "What do you know about the other rogues' plans?" he put in.

She shivered again, jerking her head away from the blast of my flames, but she couldn't resist their burn. "There were plans being made around the feline estate," she gasped out. "I don't know what. But they were preparing for something big if we failed here."

Something big. Orion has said the rest of the rogues were prepared to launch a heavy assault. How many of them were left now?

I heaved another stream of flames over the bobcat shifter, ignoring the pinching sensation that was starting to work through my muscles.

"Specifics," Marco said. "Tell us everything you know about those plans."

"That *is* all I know." Her voice turned into a whimper.

Aaron made a gesture to Nate, maybe realizing that my strength was waning. The bear shifter grabbed the rogue woman and hauled her out of the truth-searing fire.

Thomas and Alice were ready with their captive. The gawky albatross shifter flinched beneath the flames, but he didn't have any more answers to the alpha's questions than the bobcat shifter had. My throat started to throb. I gestured to my mates, and West shot out one last inquiry.

"Your allies who ran away from this attack—where would they have gone?"

"I'm not sure," the guy said in a strained voice. "Maybe to meet up with the main group in Florida?"

My flames sputtered out. My shift sputtered out too. I shrank into my human body and immediately launched into a coughing fit. Very smooth.

When I got control of my lungs, Nate's people were already hauling the two captured rogues away. "What are you going to do with them?" I asked.

"Hold them, drugged, until we decide what punishment they should face." Nate sighed. "They were only lackeys. I'd banish them—but they were outside the kin already, and look what they got up to."

Our prisoners hadn't known enough. I'd gone all the way up a mountain to earn the power of those violet flames, the ones that burned through to the truth. No other dragon shifter before me had claimed Sunridge's secret. But it still hadn't been enough to win the day.

"It sounds like as far as they knew the group that's waiting in Florida, that's most of them," I pointed out. "The 'main group,' he said. That fits with what Orion told me."

"So if we can deal with the rogues there, we might have wiped up the rest of the problem," West filled in. "Which would sound a lot more hopeful if we knew where the hell in Florida they were."

"Are we still going there?"

"I think that's the best course of action we have," Aaron said. "The rogues don't know what we've found out. We should go on to the feline estate, act as if we don't suspect anything is wrong, and investigate from there."

"And when I find out which of my kin has been

entertaining those lunatics, you'd better believe the fur is going to fly," Marco said, baring his teeth in a fierce grin.

Nate turned. His gaze fell on Orion's limp body. He looked to me, taking in the blood smeared over my skin. His jaw set.

"We'll deal with the rogues," he said in a voice that brooked no argument. "And the muskrat shifter will have a funeral with all the respect he's due."

CHAPTER 12

Aaron

Riding in an airplane never felt quite right. The whole time I was off the ground, my body never stopped itching with the awareness that I was meant to fly in other ways, not let some hunk of metal do the work for me. Given the choice, I'd almost always pick a land vehicle.

I stretched out in the leather seat, which I'd reclined as far back as it would go. I was still a little tired from spending the night before last awake and on edge, so I'd gone into the back room of the private jet on my own and drawn the curtain. So far I hadn't had a great deal of luck relaxing.

Considering the circumstances, getting to the feline estate as quickly as possible had seemed the best option. If we could deal with any rogues and their allies in Florida before they had time to finish preparing, so much the better. So I'd agreed when Nate had suggested he have one of his kin pick us up in a jet at an airfield near our ambush spot.

But even having the windows shut, the space was only shadowed, not really dark. With the thrum of the engine beneath me, I'd only been able to doze, not completely drift off. At least that had helped reduce my fatigue.

Now I was just mentally preparing myself for the events ahead of us. The feline kin and avians had never gotten on all that well, even without a traitor in the mix. Cats and birds—not a good mix.

Someone knocked against the wall outside the curtain. "Aaron?" Serenity said. "Do you mind if I join you?"

I straightened up, pushing the chair into its upright position. "Not at all. Please do."

My mate slipped past the curtain. She smiled at me, but I could see the worry and grief in her eyes. It tugged at my heart. I held my hand out to her, motioning for her to sit with me.

The seats in the back room were set up in pairs facing each other with a small table in between. Serenity sank into the one opposite me with a sigh and leaned her elbows onto the table. "Did you manage to get some rest?" she asked.

Concerned about me first, even with so much else on her mind. Every time I thought I couldn't love her more, she stole another piece of my heart. "I got enough," I said. "I think I'm ready to handle a gaggle of cats now."

Her smile twitched with amusement. "I guess they're not going to be super friendly to you, huh?"

"Doubtful. I've never actually visited the feline estate before. We've kept somewhat separate the last several years."

"Because you didn't have a dragon shifter pulling you together."

"Yes. But that time is over now." I cupped my hands around hers. "Something's bothering you. You wanted to talk to me about it?"

She bit her perfect pink lip, her amber eyes darkening. "I guess it's what you just said. The tensions between the different kin-groups. All this trouble with the rogues, and then finding out they're not just managing to sway a few of the regular kin to their side, they've got someone high up in the kin who's orchestrating attacks..."

"It's hard for all of us to accept that information," I said. "You know I didn't want to face the fact that they'd gotten to one of my kin."

She nodded. "But... you each deal with your own kin your own way. I'm supposed to somehow unite everyone. Make them all believe that, well, believing in me is the best way to go. But I hardly know them. I hardly know my own family!"

"That's not your fault. No one blames you for that."

"Well, I don't know about that," she said wryly. "I thought maybe I was getting by okay after how things went at your estate, but seeing how wary some of the disparate kin were of me—it was kind of hard to take. And I have the feeling the felines are going to be even more skeptical. They hardly trust *Marco* to lead them, and he's one of them."

I squeezed her hands, my heart squeezing too. "Look at how much you've already accomplished. You're rising to the situation better and faster than anyone could have asked, Serenity. There's more work ahead—I'm not going to pretend there isn't—but I know you can meet the challenge."

"I just..." Her gaze slid away from me. Her voice dropped. "What if trying to put things back the way they were *isn't* the best thing for all the kin? Obviously the way the rogues are trying to change things isn't right, but what if the time when dragon shifters could unify everyone is over now? Maybe it's been too long without one, and it's just causing more trouble trying to recreate the past."

"Do you really think that's true?" I asked.

"No," she said quietly. "I feel like this is where I'm meant to be. All the kin feel like my people. I want to be what all of them need. I just don't know if I can be that. And there's been so much blood shed since I came back, *because* I came back, already."

Oh, my darling mate. Taking so much responsibility onto her shoulders, more than ever should have been hers. "Come here?" I said, giving her hands a gentle tug.

She got up and sidled around the table. I eased her onto my lap, where I could look her straight in the eyes with barely any distance between us. The press of her thighs straddling mine sent a warm wash of hunger through me, but I ignored it. I brushed a lock of her hair back from her cheek. Serenity gazed down at me with affection and a little hunger of her own.

"I told you before that I've sometimes felt like an

outsider, both among the alphas and among my own kin," I said. "I know what it feels like to wonder if you're really what your people need, because they're not entirely sure you are. But from what I've seen and been through, what matters most is simply that you *are* there, that you stand up for them in every way you can whenever you can. What all the kin need right now is something stable to hold on to. You can be that sure thing they look to."

"You say that like it's easy," she said.

I chuckled. "I know it's not. But you can do it. Stay steady. Find a balance between all the demands. You've got feline cunning running through your veins, as much as you've got avian grace and canine loyalty and a bear's strength. This is what you're made for."

Ren

I bent my head even closer to Aaron's. Emotions whirled inside me. "I don't know," I said. "I don't feel all that balanced."

"No?" he murmured, raising an eyebrow.

One particular emotion was rippling through me more insistently than the rest. I wet my lips. "No. In fact, all I seem to be able to think about right now is kissing you."

My mate hummed an approving sound. "I think there's a balance we can find there too."

He traced his fingers over my cheek and met me

halfway to his mouth. If this was his demonstration, I was all for the lesson.

His tongue teased over mine and I slicked mine over his in return. My body settled lower on his lap. The bulge of his cock brushed my core through our clothes, and suddenly *that* was all I could think about.

I kissed Aaron harder, raking my fingers into his hair. He kissed me back as he gripped my waist. With a gentle tug, he fit us together perfectly.

A whimper crept from my throat. I couldn't help rocking against him, chasing the pleasure of that friction. Aaron groaned. He released my mouth to kiss a trail down my neck.

"Look at how easily we can fall into a rhythm," he murmured.

"You're my mate," I said around a hitch of breath. "We're meant for this."

He stopped and eased back to meet my eyes. "And they're your kin," he said. "All of them. They *are*. You're meant for them."

My throat choked up abruptly. I leaned my forehead against his. "I missed you so much," I said. "I know you were only gone for one night, but—"

"I know," he said, his voice thickening. "When I was stuck out there by the rogue camp, the main thing that kept me focused was thinking of you, of keeping you safe from them. I expect it'll be easier, after we've had more time together—"

"But not yet," I finished for him. "Right now, I want everything."

Desire darkened his clear blue eyes. "You can have it."

Our mouths collided again with a hot, heady kiss. Aaron's hands traveled up under my shirt to caress my breasts. I moaned into his mouth as he drew my nipples into harder peaks with each stroke of his fingers. My hips arched to meet his.

He pulled off my shirt and tossed aside my bra. Then it was his lips and his tongue teasing the tips of my breasts, one after the other.

Each nip and lick sent sparks of pleasure through me. I gasped, pressing into his embrace with a desperation I no longer felt embarrassed by. He experienced this need just as deeply as I did.

The pressure was building between my legs with a hot ache. I reached my hand between us to stroke it over his cock. Aaron's breath stuttered against my skin. He tilted his hips to give me better access.

With a jerk, I released the zipper on his slacks. My fingers slipped under the fabric of his boxers to grip him skin to skin.

"Too much clothing," I muttered.

Aaron gave a rough chuckle. "We could take care of that together too."

I lifted myself over him so he could yank my jeans and panties down my thighs. I wrenched his pants down in turn. His hand dipped between my legs, his thumb circling my clit. I gasped again, riding his fingers. But that wasn't what I really wanted to be riding.

I reached for his cock again. The way his expression softened with pleasure when I wrapped my fingers around it sent my own bliss spiraling even higher. I lowered myself onto him, moaning as he filled me.

"Serenity," Aaron whispered, like a prayer. He thrust up into me, sending a deeper wave of pleasure through me. I rocked in time with his rhythm, the ecstasy building as fast as I could follow it.

We matched each other's movements, setting the pace alongside each other. I didn't know if he was completely right about my greater role, but this? This passion couldn't have come more naturally to me.

My eagle shifter pulled me into another kiss. His hand returned to my breast, stroking it with each pump of his hips. I ran my hand down his chest as if I could grasp even more of the heat between us. The delicious burn inside me expanded, flooding all my senses.

I bucked faster, flying higher. Aaron thrust even deeper, and I plummeted over the edge into total bliss.

I kept riding him, my orgasm trembling through me, but it only took that sudden clenching to bring him past the point of no return too. He choked out a sound of release as he spent himself inside me.

I sagged against him, loving the feel of his hot, sweat-slick skin against mine. The salty, musky smell of him. He folded his arms around me, cradling me to him, and kissed my forehead.

"And any time you need another demonstration..." he said.

I laughed and hugged him tightly. I still wasn't sure I was ready for whatever waited for us up ahead, but at least I'd be facing it with my mates.

CHAPTER 13

Ren

I'D ALREADY DONE the arriving at an alpha's estate thing twice now. I shouldn't have felt so nervous. But as the private jet touched down on the fringes of the feline kin property just south of Miami, my stomach balled into one huge knot.

It wasn't just the new kin group I had to meet. It was the traitor we already knew was lurking among the prominent families. And maybe there was more than one. Orion hadn't been all that involved with the rogues. There had to be plenty they hadn't let him in on.

Marco had called a few of his estate's security people ahead of time to meet us at the airfield. "They'll give us the all clear when they've taken a thorough look around the perimeter," he said.

West leaned back in his chair, his shoulders tensed. "And you're sure we can trust *them*?"

Marco narrowed his eyes at the wolf shifter, but he

smiled at the same time. "I trust that they're not *all* traitors, and the ones who aren't will catch anything that needs catching."

My phone's ringtone started playing, so unexpectedly I flinched in my seat. My mates all shot curious glances my way. No one had this number other than Kylie. I fumbled for the phone and answered it as quickly as I could.

"Kylie, what's up? Is something wrong?"

"Not at all!" her cheerful voice rang out on the other end. "Everything is spectacular. Especially because I just touched down in Miami. So how exactly do I get from the airport to this shifter estate of yours?"

I blinked, my mind going momentarily blank. "Um, what?"

"I flew down to see you! You said you were going to be near Miami, and there was a sale going on—the flight was *so* cheap. I couldn't resist."

I opened and closed my mouth a few times before I managed to produce more words. "Okay. Okay. Oh my God. Let me just... talk to the guys."

Who were all still watching me. Marco looked amused, Aaron curious, Nate concerned, and West— well, it was pretty hard to read West's expression at certain moments. I'd go with "grim" this time around.

Marco was the man to deal with logistics here, I guessed. I muffled the phone with my palm. "Kylie, uh, flew herself down here. She's at the Miami airport. Can we... bring her here? She wants to visit."

"I'm not sure now is the best time for that," Aaron pointed out.

Oh. Right. In my shock, I'd completely forgotten that even we weren't necessarily safe on the estate. And Kylie didn't have any shifter super powers to call on if the situation went south. A chill trickled through me. "She's already here. I don't know if she can even afford to change her ticket to go right back."

Marco was already waving his hand dismissively. "Don't even think about that. We can cover whatever you need."

I got back on the phone. "Actually, Kylie... We're in kind of a bad place right now. We found out that one of Marco's people has been helping the rogues, and it sounds like they're planning an attack while we're here. I don't want you getting hurt again, even though I do really, really want to see you."

There was a pause. "You're worried I'll be in the way," Kylie said. Sounding truly downcast was outside her vocal range, but I could hear her disappointment in the flattening of her enthusiasm.

"No!" I said. "I just know, if there's fighting or something, you can't defend yourself the same way."

Kylie sucked in a breath. "What if I'm okay with that?" she said. "I've survived a long time around people a lot bigger and tougher than me. I'm not going to be a liability, Ren. Maybe I'll even help! I found that first clue of your mom's for you." She paused again. "Unless you just don't want me there at all."

My heart wrenched. I did want to have her with me, to talk to her face to face instead of via a phone screen, so badly. Kylie *had* survived an awful lot in the city during the years we'd been on the streets. Maybe I was underestimating just how strong—and resourceful—a non-shifter could be.

"I do," I said quickly. "Believe me, I do. You're right. I'll get Marco to send somebody. When I know what the plan is, I'll text you any details you'll need."

As I hung up, Marco arched his eyebrow at me. I sagged in my seat. "She made a very compelling argument. And Kylie is the toughest person I know, even if she doesn't look it."

"It's up to you, princess," Marco said. "I can send someone."

I waited for one of the other alphas—probably West—to argue, but no one did. "Okay. When you send them off, let me know where Kylie should meet them."

Marco nodded. Then he swept his arm expansively toward the bunch of us. "We're good to go now. My staff have prepared an informal luncheon-slash-meet-and-greet. I'd tell you to behave yourselves, but my kin probably won't, so just do as you see fit."

Alice fell into step with me as we headed for the plane's door. "I'll keep an extra eye on your friend if you want."

My eyes widened. "If it's any trouble—"

"None," she said firmly. "Friends are important. Lord knows you're going to need as many as you can get, and I don't see any point in discriminating about who or what they are. If she's important to you, that's good enough for me."

I smiled at her, more touched than I knew how to say. Apparently I'd made at least one more solid friend during my time with the shifter kin.

Marco's estate was farther inland than Aaron's, but the salt in the breeze told me there was a brackish lake nearby. Otherwise the place felt totally different from either of the other estates I'd visited. Lush tropical vegetation grew all around the paths, palm trees shading us with their fronds overhead. The summer heat had a damp weight to it.

The house, when we reached it, was a massive colonial mansion, all peach except the ornate white trim around the windows and doors. A greenhouse almost the same size as the rest of the building, its glass tinted to prevent anyone from looking in, jutted from the northern wing.

Having stayed briefly in one of the feline alpha's guesthouses, I knew what to expect from the inside of the mansion: thick rugs, Victorian antique furnishings, and velvet basically everywhere. I felt underdressed the second I walked in the door. Marco led the way to the expansive ballroom where his "informal luncheon" was taking place.

A few dozen feline shifters—the ones who lived on the estate grounds, I assumed—were already gathered there, snacking on tidbits from the platters set on tables along the walls. Most of them glanced our way, but no one hurried over to greet us.

Typical cat aloofness, I found myself thinking, and caught myself before I smirked. Yeah, the feline shifters certainly kept to the attitudes of their animal counterparts.

But one of the kin around me might be scheming

right now to overthrow all of us. I studied each of them as Marco ushered me deeper into the room.

"Alpha," a woman in the first group we approached said, with the slightest bob of her head in deference. Her scent told me she was a lion. She turned her golden eyes on me. "And this is the dragon shifter." Her tone gave away no clear emotion, but I felt her sizing me up. I lifted my chin instinctively, wishing I'd insisted on changing into something more elegant than jeans and a T-shirt.

"This is the great Serenity herself," Marco said languidly but without any hint of irony. "I hope all of my kin will make her feel welcome."

"Naturally," the lion shifter said. She offered an elegant hand for me to shake. "Coreen of the Bushnells."

"A pleasure to meet you," I said, biting back any other comments I might have made about the warmth of her welcome—or lack thereof.

The other introductions went pretty much the same way. A cryptic remark, a once-over, a mild show of respect. The feline kin were definitely a lot different from the other shifters I'd met. I didn't get hostile vibes from any of them, but really, it was hard to tell who might have been simply unaffected and who outright dismissive.

"Are they always like this?" I murmured to Marco when we stopped by one of the tables for a moment alone. "Or are they insulting you—or me—or someone?"

He chuckled. "Princess, this is about as enthusiastic for leadership as my kin ever get. I'm actually impressed." His head turned, and he sighed. "Well, I was. Prepare yourself."

For what? I wanted to ask, but the problem he'd seen coming was already on us.

"*Well* then," purred the lynx shifter who'd sidled up at my right. I couldn't tell whether the flecks of silver in his tawny hair were part of his animal's coloring or a reflection of age, but if he was any more than thirty-five, he wore the years well. He gave me a sly grin as he considered me. "Aren't you the loveliest shifter I've ever seen walk in that door. No offense meant to my alpha."

He winked at Marco, who smiled indulgently. "None taken, Silvan. I know exactly how lovely I am without you buttering me up."

"Perhaps while you're busy with your duties, I could take this treasure on a tour of the estate." Silvan's attention came back to me. His voice practically dripped with flirtation. "There are so *many* things I could show you."

I'd bet there were. I clamped my jaw, not sure whether I was more likely to laugh or sputter in indignation. Was he seriously propositioning me right in front of my mate?

Marco didn't seem to care—but then, Marco made a habit of appearing not to care about anything. And maybe this guy thought he could get away with the flirtation because his alpha *wasn't* fully my mate yet.

Any good humor I'd been feeling about the encounter died. I gave the lynx shifter a firm stare. "I appreciate the offer, but I know Marco will look after me just fine." I tucked my hand around Marco's elbow at the same time. My jaguar shifter didn't say anything, but I felt a tremor of pleased energy travel through his posture.

Silvan seemed unfazed. "Well, if you should change your mind, I'm sure you can find me." He sauntered off.

"Wow," I said. "That was... something."

"I should probably warn you that you're likely to get at least three similar offers before the day is over," Marco said. His smile turned crooked.

A murmur rose up near the doorway at the far end of the ballroom. I glanced over, and my gaze caught in a shock of neon pink hair. My heart leapt.

"Kylie!"

I dashed across the room, suddenly glad I wasn't dressed up, because I could move a heck of a lot faster in sneakers than heels. My best friend squealed when she saw me. We threw our arms around each other, me being careful not to squeeze her *too* hard with my newfound dragon strength. Not that Kylie was any lightweight. She was small, yeah, but full of wiry toughness.

When I let her go, she looked around the room, her eyes sparkling. "This is freaking amazing, Ren. And I thought Marco's place in New York was posh. So this is, like, the capital of cat shifters?"

I grinned. "Something like that. I can't believe you're here! How long can you stay?"

"I'm supposed to be back at work on Tuesday, but I can always call in. I haven't used any sick days yet. Oh my God! I'm going to get to see you be a dragon." She grasped my hands, and we spun around in an excited little dance. "Where are those hunks of yours, anyway?"

I looked up and realized we'd become the center of attention. The shifters all around the room were staring at me and my bestie—well, mostly at my bestie. One woman's nostril's flared.

"Why has a *human* been allowed into our estate?" she demanded.

I stepped closer to Kylie automatically, my hackles rising. Marco strode over with an air of authority I'd rarely seen him emit. But then, this was the first time I'd seen him among so many of his kin.

"The human is your dragon shifter's ally," he said, pitching his voice loud enough for the whole room to hear. "And you will treat her with the same respect you would a dragon. Any arguments?" He offered a sharp smile.

Several heads turned away. The other stares lowered. The woman who'd complained muttered something, and Marco said, in a soft, clear voice, "What was that, Livia?"

Her lips pressed flat, her face paling slightly. "Nothing, sir."

Marco didn't look convinced, but he let it slide. "A surprise visit, but a welcome one," he said to Kylie as he joined us.

Kylie's expression had gone a bit tight. "It's not going to be a big deal that I'm here, is it? Everyone seemed so chill in the other shifter village, I didn't think they'd get upset."

"They'll get over it. We felines are very adaptable." The smile he gave her was a lot warmer than the one he'd offered the crowd.

"Come on," I said, grabbing Kylie's arm. "You've got to be hungry. They've got *everything* to eat here." I kept my tone chipper even though my heart was thudding.

Alice caught my eye from across the room, and I nodded. I was definitely going to want her to have my best friend's back around this bunch.

We'd only made it partway to the tables when a new voice boomed across the room. "Alpha! If you even deserve that title."

Bristling, I pivoted on my feet. A hulking tiger shifter was stalking toward Marco, his head high and eyes lit with menace. The guy must have had at least half a foot and fifty pounds on my jaguar shifter.

A prickle ran over my skin as my body instinctively readied to shift. I held myself back. It wasn't going to help Marco's case if his mate fought his battles for him.

"Julius," Marco said blandly. "What are you nattering about now?"

The tiger shifter came to a halt a few feet from his alpha and scowled. "I say you're not strong enough to lead us all. I say a real alpha would have consummated his bond with the dragon, not stepped aside while other kin's leaders did, leaving all of us still waiting. I say I could crush you with one blow of my paws."

My skin went cold. The other shifters had fallen completely silent, even more still than when Kylie had arrived. Marco folded his arms over his chest and cocked his head. "Is that a formal challenge, or just bluster?"

"Consider yourself challenged," Julius growled. "Tonight, unless you're going to try to weasel your way out of it."

"No weaseling necessary," Marco said lightly. "I'll be happy to settle this tonight. May the best kin win."

CHAPTER 14

Ren

KYLIE LOOPED her arm around mine as an attendant led us down the hall to our rooms. She pitched her voice low. "So... this whole challenge thing. What exactly does that mean for Marco?"

I swallowed hard. My pulse hadn't stopped racing since the tiger shifter had swaggered out of the ballroom. I wished I had a better idea what the challenge had meant myself.

"I'm not sure," I said. "The other guy wants the alpha position. I guess they fight it out. Tonight." In, what, just a few hours? Marco couldn't have been prepared for that.

Was *this* what being alpha had been like for him all along? Random challenges at every turn, not even being able to spend an hour back on his estate without some asshole confronting him? That would get old awfully quick. Suddenly I didn't find it hard to believe he'd meant the comment he'd made about giving up the position.

Only he couldn't do that and still be my mate. If he forfeited his position as alpha, my bond would shift to whoever was named in his place.

And the same if he lost this challenge.

"But he'll be fine, right?" Kylie said. "I mean, he's stayed on top this long."

"Yeah," I said. If only I felt totally confident of Marco's victory. In the back of my mind, I kept seeing the tiger shifter standing over him, taller and broader. Size wasn't everything—but it mattered a hell of a lot in a fight.

"Geez. I had no idea things would be this tense. I'm sorry if I made the situation any worse."

"Hey." I pulled Kylie around to face me as the attendant opened a door for her. "I'm glad you're here. Any trouble Marco's kin make is their fault, not yours. Thank you for coming. Just having you with me makes everything feel a little easier to handle."

My best friend beamed at me and pulled me into another hug. "That's why I'm here."

I hugged her back, and then stepped away. "I do still want you staying safe, though. Can you just, like hole up in your guest room for a little while. I think I should talk to Marco."

Kylie waved me off. "Of course, of course. Go tend to your 'mate.' I can already see I've got plenty of luxury in here to keep me occupied. But if you run into any handsome unoccupied shifters, feel free to send them my way too!"

I couldn't help laughing, even though my stomach was still tight. "I'll do that."

Marco's private rooms were just down the hall from mine. I knocked. "Marco?"

"Come in," he called from the other side. When I stepped in, he was standing by the chaise lounge in the sitting room. He shot me an amused glance. "You don't need to knock with me, princess. Consider these rooms as much yours as they are mine."

"I'll keep that in mind. Are you okay?"

Marco shrugged with a careless air, but I knew him well enough now to notice the angry glint in his indigo eyes. "Challenges happen. They have before and will again. It isn't how I would have hoped to spend my first evening here with you, but we'll just have to make tomorrow night even better to make up for it."

His grin looked a little tense too. I walked up to him. "It sounded like that Julius guy had been a pain in the ass before now."

Marco nodded. "He likes to hear himself talk, especially if it's to complain about how anyone else is doing things. Apparently he's decided to graduate from talking."

"Do you think he's the one allied with the rogues?" I asked.

"It could be. A challenge, if he succeeded, would be a fairly direct way to disrupt the status quo. But he's not going to succeed, so really it's a very bad plan, if it is one."

Julius had radiated aggressive disdain, but there was no way for me to tell whether that feeling was simply personal or whether he had a larger agenda. It didn't really matter anyway. It didn't change what I'd come here to do.

I touched Marco's face, tracing my fingers along the line of his angular jaw. "I guess we could enjoy ourselves before tomorrow evening too."

A different sort of light sparked in Marco's eyes. He dipped his head close to mine. "What exactly did you have in mind, my Princess of Flames?"

I kissed him in answer. He hummed low in his throat and kissed me back, his hands rising to tangle in my hair. The graze of his fingers over my scalp left my whole body tingling in anticipation.

He tilted my head slightly to deepen the kiss. I pressed my mouth to his hungrily. The bond inside me thrummed with eagerness, urging me on.

Without breaking the kiss, I stepped backward through the doorway into the bedroom. Marco followed. His tongue teased into my mouth, and for one hot, heady moment it sparred with mine. Then I had to let go of him to hop up on the bed.

Marco prowled after me, nothing but longing in his gaze now. He bent over me on the bed and claimed my mouth again. His fingers brushed over my breasts with just enough pressure to pebble my nipples through my shirt and bra—but not half as much as I was dying for. I arched into his touch, and he chuckled breathlessly.

"All in good time," he murmured on his way into another kiss.

No. The more time we took, the more opportunity he had to question my motivations.

I grasped his shirt and tugged it up. Marco let me peel it off, staying poised over me for a few seconds as I drank in his lean chest. I ran my hands over the planes of solid muscle, and his eyelids dipped.

"Princess," he said in a hungry growl.

I pulled my shirt off too. Marco leaned in to kiss his way down the side of my neck and across my collarbone. I whimpered when he reached the boundary of my bra. To my relief, he made short work of that obstacle. With a quick gesture, he'd unhooked it and tossed it aside. Then he was slicking his tongue over one needy nipple.

I gasped at the rush of pleasure spreading through my chest. Yes, this was exactly what we both needed. One of my arms looped around Marco's shoulders. The other crept down my body to undo the fly of my jeans. I caught Marco's hand and guided it along the same path.

He groaned when his fingers reached the dampness on my panties. I shivered with longing, the ache between my legs only growing as he stroked me there.

"So determined," Marco said in a low, amused voice. He paused, his hand going still. His eyes sought out mine. His expression had turned abruptly serious. "Princess, what are you doing?"

Shit. "Seducing you?" I said with all the coyness I could manage, fluttering my eyelashes at him. "Is that a problem?"

He withdrew his hand completely. I almost moaned at the loss of contact. He set it on the other side of my body and lifted himself so he was staring down at me.

"Why now?"

"Does it matter? I want you, you want me..." I teased my fingers down his bare chest to the waist of his jeans.

Marco closed his eyes for a second as if gathering his

self-control. When he looked at me again, his gaze was stark. "Ren. Please. Why *now*?"

I couldn't bear to lie to my mate, not when he asked me like that. I swallowed hard. "I do want you. But I also... Julius took a jab at you because our bond isn't consummated yet. I thought if it was, maybe he'd back down."

"Oh, princess." Marco let his head drop until his nose almost grazed mine. "Do you really think I'll lose to that sorry excuse for a tiger?"

"No," I said, mostly honestly. The images that had haunted me since Julius had first spoken his challenge floated back into my head. All the ways I might find Marco after the battle, battered and bleeding. "I don't want to see how badly he might hurt you while you're winning. If I can save you from that..."

Marco sucked in a breath. "There was a time not long ago when I thought you might enjoy seeing me batted around some."

My back stiffened. The idea that I'd wish that kind of pain on him wrenched at me so hard tears sprang into my eyes. "No," I choked out. "I was angry at you, but I would never want—that's the last thing I—"

Marco's eyes had widened. He brushed his thumb over my lips, stopping my struggle for words. "I'm sorry," he said. "It was only a joke—a bad one, clearly. I... didn't realize my wellbeing meant so much to you."

"Of course it does, you idiot," I muttered. "You're my mate. You're obviously upset about the challenge. I just thought, this is the one thing I can do that might help..."

"Serenity." Marco lowered himself on his side next to

me and tugged me against him. He kissed my forehead, his voice a little shaky. "You have no idea how much you've helped already, with everything you'd done so far. And I'm not upset about the challenge because I'm afraid of Julius. Confrontations like that—they just stir up memories I'd rather avoid."

I nestled my head against his shoulder. "Like what?"

He hesitated for a long moment. When he spoke again, his voice was even quieter. "You've asked me before how I got this scar." He touched the pale line that bisected his eyebrow. "I told you it was from a challenge. That particular challenge... came from a kin-member I'd considered a friend. One of my closest friends. We'd grown up together, played and trained together before I was even named next alpha-in-line. I'd have fought to the death for him."

My throat had gone tight. Oh, God. "But instead you had to fight to the death *against* him."

"Not to the death. Not in that moment. But I had to fight him, yes. I had to hear him tell me he didn't believe I deserved to be alpha, that I didn't deserve to even be kin, and then I had to beat him into submission." Marco paused with a hissed inhale. "It was him or me, and in the end I chose me."

"You did what you had to do."

"Yes. But when there's a challenge, the loser is banished. An alpha can't have someone who tried to undermine our authority just hanging around. And Devon didn't know what to do with himself once he was out on his own."

"What happened?" I asked. I could already tell from

the weight in Marco's voice that it wasn't good.

"He ended up tangling with a bunch of vampires. They were *really* not pleased about whatever he said or did to them." Marco swallowed audibly. "When we found his body... it was obvious they'd tortured him for a while before they'd finished the job. So no, I didn't kill him. But I did send him to his death. And the worst death I can imagine."

I wrapped my arm around my mate, hugging him. "You didn't have a choice. You couldn't have known what would happen to him. It's not as if you made him mess with those vampires."

"I tell myself all that," Marco said. "But I still feel like I've been punched in the gut every time I hear the words of a challenge."

I drank in the smell of his skin, like spiced coffee. The stutter of his breath. The tension still wound through his muscles. He hadn't wanted to tell me that story. He'd avoided it for weeks. But he had, finally, so that I'd understand.

"That's why you were impatient to consummate," I said. "Why it was so important to you to secure your position any way you could."

"I shouldn't have seen you that way," Marco said quickly. "I didn't *want* to think about you that way. But the thought was there. I let it get to me. You know how sorry I am for that."

"But now—" I started, moving my body against his.

Marco groaned, but he gripped my thigh to hold me still. "Ren, tell me the truth. Would you be offering right now if Julius *hadn't* challenged me?"

I wanted to say yes. The word caught in my throat. I couldn't know exactly what I'd have done if the luncheon had played out differently... but I could make a reasonable guess.

"That's what I thought," Marco said at my hesitation.

"Marco..."

He cupped my face, gazing into my eyes. "Princess, it's okay. The first time we go there, I want it to be only because you want it, not even slightly because circumstances are forcing your hand. I can beat Julius without breaking a sweat, and I can wait. It's the least I can do."

I choked up again, but for a completely different reason. The fact that he was saying no had dissolved the last of my doubts. I could have given myself over happily now, looming challenge or not.

But I'd already burned that bridge for the moment. I settled for kissing him, soft and sweet, as his hand stroked over the side of my face.

My body was still tingling with longing. Maybe Marco could feel that too. He drew back a couple of inches with a sly smile. "I would, however, be happy to enjoy you in another way."

Before I had to ask what he meant, he was easing down my body. His fingers hooked the hem of my panties as he brushed his lips over my breasts and belly. I gasped when his mouth closed over the bundle of nerves at my core. Every part of my brain that had been cycling through worries short-circuited, and for a brief moment in time, I was made of nothing but bliss.

CHAPTER 15

West

I NEVER FELT REALLY comfortable around feline shifters. Marco I could put up with, because at least he was dedicated to something. The rest of his kin—you never knew what was going on behind those shifty eyes.

At least, most of them read as shifty. The tiger shifter who'd challenged Marco a couple hours ago came across as a pretty straight-forward asshole. Or that's what I'd determined while I'd been keeping an eye on him. Right now he was playing pool with a couple of his kin in the estate's big entertainment room, bellowing victory whenever he hit a ball into a pocket. The sound made me wince inwardly even from across the room. I adjusted my position against the wall near the door.

I had my phone out, pretending I was mostly paying attention to that. I had actually checked in with a few of my lieutenants while Julius the Tiger had swaggered and blustered. Now I was playing a very half-hearted game of

Candy Crush while keeping my ears perked to the conversations around me.

I'd just cleared a level when Ren strode past me into the room. A whiff of her scent reached my nose: the usual sweetness mingled with a musk that got me half-hard in two seconds flat. I straightened up, resisting the urge to lick my lips. And ignoring the twist of jealousy in my chest. She'd just been with at least one of the other alphas —I knew that much. And that alpha had gotten her off, well.

One hint of the smell of arousal on her, and I was right back to the other night in her bed. My mouth on her skin, her hand around my cock—

Yeah, thinking about that right now wasn't going to take me anywhere useful. I dragged in a breath to steady the thump of my pulse.

Our dragon shifter wasn't here to see me. She marched right across the room and came to a stop by the pool table, her gaze fixed on Julius. Shit. What the hell was she up to now?

I shoved my phone into my pocket and ambled a little closer, trying to look casual, which wasn't easy when every feline shifter nearby glanced over at the scent of wolf. Julius turned and spotted Ren. He set his pool stick against the floor, grinning.

"Dragon shifter. Come to get an early start with your new mate?"

Ren's chin rose higher, her eyes flashing. She looked fucking gorgeous like that, but it also meant she was about to throw herself right in over her head. So damned determined to right every wrong even when she barely understood the threat she was facing. It wrenched at my heart, but that sense of justice wasn't going to do anyone any good if she got torn to pieces in the process. I tensed, ready to shift.

"No," Ren said, clear and loud enough that the whole room had to hear. "I came to give you an out. Marco is going to win tonight. And even if he wasn't going to, I'd never accept *you* as my mate. I thought it was only fair to mention that ahead of time."

The tiger shifter's face darkened. His lips curled into more of a sneer. "Is that what our alpha is reduced to now? Sending you to protect him while he hides in his rooms?"

Ren rolled her eyes. "No. *He's* happy to put you in your place the regular way. But I'd rather not see any kin banished when they don't need to be. Consider it a courtesy. There's no point in pursuing a lost cause."

Julius rapped the end of his pool cue against the floor. His eyes had narrowed. "I don't think it's lost at all. And I think you'll find it a lot harder to say no when the bond passes to me."

Ren looked him up and down, letting every hint of her disdain show in her expression. Oh, Lord, she was aiming to get herself eviscerated, wasn't she?

"Believe me," she said flippantly. "I can't imagine even being tempted."

Julius bristled, baring his teeth. "We'll see if you change your tune after tonight, won't we? Or maybe you need to learn your place now."

"I know my place," Ren said. "And it happens to be very far over yours. But if that's how you're going to act,

I'll enjoy watching you get your ass handed to you tonight."

She swiveled and headed back toward the doorway. Julius's arm jerked as if he meant to lunge after her, and I braced myself to leap between them. But he caught himself with a harsh inhale. His gaze tracked Ren to the door with an angry, predatory gleam.

I waited just long enough to make sure he was staying put, and then I strode after my mate.

~

Ren

My pulse was thudding as I walked out of the games room, but the second I crossed the threshold into the hall, my lips stretched into a smile. The *look* on Julius's face when I'd told him what was what—I was going to treasure that for a good long time.

I didn't get to savor my victory very long in the moment. I'd hardly made it two more steps when a hand closed around my forearm. A hint of pine laced the air. I knew my confronter was West before he spun me around to face him.

"What the hell were you trying to pull in there?" he snapped, his gaze in full glower mode. "That tiger shifter just about bit your head off."

I guffawed. "I'd have liked to see him try. He'd have been fried cat before he even got his teeth in."

"You're still learning control over your shifts. And

you don't know these kin at all. You can't take risks like that."

"I don't know. Seems like I just did, and the world didn't end."

West let out a strangled sound. Suddenly his hand was on the side of my neck, his thumb tracing my jaw as he yanked me closer to him. His head bowed close to mine. His body was just inches away, so close it was almost an embrace. Every nerve in *my* body woke up in response. I breathed in his pine-forest scent and held myself back from turning my face that slight distance to kiss him. Let him make the first move here, when he figured out what he wanted.

His breath spilled hot and harsh over my cheek. His grip on my arm loosened. For a second, I thought he was going to grasp my waist and pull me flush against him. And whatever happened after that, I was pretty sure I'd be on board for.

Instead, his shoulders tensed. "Listen to me. Don't *ever* do anything that stupid again."

The rush of attraction faded. I gritted my teeth and shoved West back a step with my free hand. "I wasn't being *stupid*," I bit out, keeping my voice low. "But it's nice to know you still see me as an idiot. I was provoking Julius on purpose. I wanted to get a better sense of his emotions, and those of the other kin in the room, to figure out who might be allied with the rogues."

West's expression blanked. "What?"

"I can read people better when their emotions are on the surface," I said. "So I wanted to stir things up. He wasn't even close to trying to actually hurt me. I'd have felt it if he was."

"Oh." West deflated slightly. His fingers flexed around my arm. He looked down at them, into the space between us still narrow enough that I could feel the heat emanating from his body. "Are you so sure your senses work as well on shifters as the human beings you're used to, Sparks? Because you haven't really had much chance for practice."

"I can read you just fine," I muttered. "And right now you should be feeling a lot more embarrassed than you actually are, just FYI. Although I appreciate the not-wanting-me-to-get-hurt side of this whole outburst."

West grimaced. He raised his eyes again. There might have been a shadow of an apology in them, but he didn't bother to voice it. "Did you find out anything useful with all your 'stirring up'?"

"That depends on how you define useful. Julius has something motivating him other than just wanting the alpha position. I didn't get the sense he even considered backing down. Whether he wins or not, whether I accept him as a mate or not if he does win, the challenge is about more than that. Enough more that the rest doesn't matter."

"More as in he expects it to work into his plans with the rogues?"

"That would be my best guess." I frowned, thinking about the vibes I'd felt around me in the room. "I don't think anyone else who was in the room is involved. His kin were curious about what was going on, but none of them gave the impression of feeling at all threatened by me telling him off. Or angry. They just found it entertaining. Anyone who was in on a plot, I think they'd have cared more."

West nodded. "That reasoning seems sound." He raised an eyebrow. "Maybe your gambit gave us some results after all."

"Maybe next time you should ask me what I'm doing before assuming I'm being an idiot."

"Maybe you should stop coming up with plans that *look* idiotic."

I bit my lip, swallowing my frustration, and West's gaze dropped to my mouth. The heat between us flared in an instant. God almighty, why did he have to act like a jerk when I knew there was so much compassion—not to mention plain old passion—underneath that front?

Every muscle was urging me to just grab him and plant one on him. To draw out the desire I knew he was keeping locked down inside.

But we'd gone down that road already, and that blazing physical encounter hadn't made things any better. Actually, the moment we'd shared in the avian estate garden had only made me more on edge when I was with him, now that I knew how good the two of us could be together.

This game of snarking at each other and dancing around our attraction was getting old. I was ready to be done with it, one way or the other.

I turned my hand, sliding it against his arm until my fingers could curl around his. "West," I said, "I think we should talk. *Really* talk. We're not getting anywhere like this. Whatever doubts you still have about me, you can just tell me about them. We'll hash them out. I know I'm still learning here. But I need to know what the problem is before I can fix it."

The sense I got from my wolf shifter then was completely bizarre, as if a rush of tangled emotions had blown open a door inside him—only to be yanked back in and the door slammed shut. And deadbolted for good measure.

West took another step back, his posture rigid. His hand slipped from mine. "I don't think this is exactly the time for chatting, Sparks," he said. "We've got a full-blown rebellion to stop."

And for some reason you're just as important to me as stopping it, you blockhead, I thought but didn't let myself say. I'd had my fill of verbal sparring for the day.

"Fine," I said. "When you get your head sorted out, you know where to find me." I turned and stalked away without a backward glance. Because I did have bigger things to think about up ahead. Like whether one of my other mates was going to come out of tonight's confrontation with all limbs and vital organs intact.

CHAPTER 16

Ren

THE GUEST SUITE Kylie had been given looked a lot like my set of rooms, other than her bed was only a regular king sized one and not wide enough to comfortably fit five. I guessed the shifter kin didn't expect anyone other than their dragon shifter to be calling multiple mates into their bed. Or else they expected those other people to squish.

"Is everything settled now?" Kylie asked me, bobbing on her feet. She'd only managed to sit on the elegant settee for about ten seconds before she'd bounced back up again with her irresistible energy.

"As settled as it can be," I said. "Marco still has to fight that guy. But he seems sure he can take him. I just hope he's prepared for anything. The rogues definitely don't mind fighting dirty."

"They haven't tried anything that big so far, though, right?" Kylie said. "I mean, there were the three that attacked us at West's people's village, and then it sounded like you took on that bunch near Nate's estate no problem."

My heart sank with the weight of all the things I'd been avoiding telling her. I should have told her everything sooner. Maybe if she'd realized just how dangerous my life had gotten, she wouldn't have rushed down here on this visit.

On the other hand, maybe she'd just have rushed down sooner.

"There've been a couple of other... incidents," I said, slowly. "When we were traveling to Sunridge, a bunch of them ambushed us. That was when I managed a full shift the first time. And the rogues who attacked Nate's estate —they killed four of the kin before the guards managed to stop them."

"Oh!" Kylie's eyes went wide. "The thing at Sunridge—that was weeks ago. Why didn't you tell me?"

I worried my lower lip with my teeth. My fingers shivered with an itch I hadn't felt in days—the urge to find some object to pilfer, to take control. I curled them into my palm instead. I wasn't that street rat thief anymore. I was a freaking dragon shifter now.

"I knew you'd be worried," I said. "We came out of the ambush fine, and the attack on the estate was over before I even got there."

Kylie was still looking at me with a hesitant expression. "I'd rather be worried and know what's really going on with you than be kept in the dark. You should know that, Ren."

I had. But I'd kept her in the dark anyway. There wasn't really any way I could justify it.

"I'm sorry," I said. "There was so much going on... Keeping quiet about it and focusing on the good stuff just felt like the best way of handling it at the time. But you see why *I'm* worried."

Kylie nodded. "I guess if those asshole rogues do turn up, you can go full dragon mode on their assess," she said, more of her usual cheerfulness coming back.

"That's the plan." I groped for a change in subject—to a subject that wouldn't make me want to pocket every valuable in the building. "Marco's people will be summoning us to dinner soon. I should put on something nicer. If there are rogues around, I want them remembering who's in charge here." I managed to grin. "You want to help me pick out a dress?"

"Want to?" Kylie said, clapping her hands. "I've been dying to since you sent me that photo of you at Aaron's place. All right, let's do this thing."

We ducked into the hall and passed a few doors to my rooms.

I opened one wardrobe and then another. Kylie made a squeeing sound as she pawed through the offerings. "Oh, this is amazing. You're going to look like a boss, all right. Forget princess—you're going to be the empress of all shifters."

I laughed and held out my arms to take the first dress she tossed to me. By the time she'd gone through all three wardrobes, my arms were aching and my face buried in silk and satin. I hefted the heap onto the bed. "Um, I think we need to do a little narrowing down here."

"Yes, yes." Kylie tapped her lips. She grabbed a couple out of the pile. "I don't know what I was thinking with this one. And now that I'm looking at them all, black is definitely too dour. The rest you'll just have to put on so I can ogle you."

She shot me a bright smile as she went to put back the discards. I shook my head and stripped out of my T-shirt and jeans. As I shimmied into one of the dresses from the top of the heap, a simple pale green silk number, Kylie sat down on the edge of the bed. She glanced across its width, her eyebrows arching in amusement. "Hmm, I can't imagine what you'd need a bed *this* big for... No, wait, actually I can."

My face flushed at her teasing. But when she turned back to me, a shadow had crossed her face.

"Is there anything else you decided not to tell me from the last few weeks?" she asked.

Shit. I looked at myself in the mirror, contemplating the green silk flowing over my body. Did I look like an ingénue or a girl who'd severely fucked up the best friendship she'd ever had? Neither was what I was going for. I reached to pull that one off.

"There might have been a few things," I admitted without meeting Kylie's eyes. "Not that I didn't want you to know. Just that would have been hard to talk about with only texts."

"You could have called me," Kylie pointed out.

"I couldn't see getting into it except face to face." Except now here we were, face to face, and I felt even more awkward. I grabbed a wine red gown out of the pile. "I told you my mom died on the mountain... I saw it. Like a vision. It was a bunch of fae who killed her. Murdered her. They were trying to stop her from getting that power she wanted me to have."

"The special fire that you can use to make people tell the truth," Kylie filled in.

"Yeah." At least I'd kept her up to speed that much.

"Why did the fae care about that?"

"I don't know," I said honestly. "Things have been tense between the shifters and the fae, but I'm still finding out the details there. Their attack wasn't, like, officially sanctioned, but the fae monarch hadn't discouraged it either. They must not have wanted any shifter to have that kind of power."

And to be fair, the first person I'd used it on was their own monarch. To be fair to *me*, I wouldn't have needed to use it on her if she'd been upfront with us in the first place.

Kylie rubbed her mouth. "Wow. So you have to worry about the fae coming after you too?"

"Not exactly. There's a treaty—and we confronted the fae monarch, and she swore to follow it. But I guess it's always possible they could decide to break their word."

That was an awful thought. I'd rather not go there while we had the rogue threat right in front of us.

"Damn." Kylie looked over at me, and her eyes lit up. Her smile looked a little stiff, but I'd take it. "And *damn*. Okay, forget all the other ones. That is The Dress."

My lips twitched. I glanced down at myself, smoothing my hands over the gleaming fabric. "Yeah?"

"Oh, yeah. Anyone who messes with you in that get-up is just asking to become dragon barbeque."

I laughed, and for a second, things between us felt almost okay. This was Kylie. My best friend, my one true friend. She'd always had my back. If I couldn't even live up to her expectations, I didn't have a hope in hell with the shifters.

"Holy cow," Kylie said when we stepped into the ballroom-turned-banquet hall. "And I thought this place couldn't get any fancier."

Marco, who was between us holding my hand, chuckled. "My kin are known for being easily distracted by shiny objects. I'm no exception."

"Well, you definitely went all out on the shiny," I said. Silver plates glinted at every seat; crystal wine glasses sparkled. Gold embroidery shimmered in a looping pattern along the edge of the gleaming white tablecloths. The crystal chandeliers overhead were all alight now, sending a sharp yellow glow over everything and everyone below.

I had a feeling it wasn't just those lights that made the feline kin look a tad jaundiced. Tension hummed through the room beneath the clamor of voices. This wasn't just a dinner. It wasn't even just their first formal dinner with their new dragon shifter in attendance. It was the dinner before their alpha's latest challenge. One that had even higher stakes than any of those before.

I nodded and smiled to the feline kin as Marco

walked me up to the head table. The other alphas were already sitting in their spots around the two chairs reserved for us. I sat down with Marco at my left and Aaron at my right. Nate leaned past the eagle shifter to catch my eyes and offer a warm smile. But my pulse had already picked up again with a prickle of anxiety.

Kylie ended up at Nate's right, which was probably the best I could have hoped for when she couldn't sit right next to me. She grinned at the big bear shifter and immediately started gabbing away. I could only imagine how West would have reacted if he'd had to be her conversation partner through dinner instead of having stoic Alice on his other side. Kylie would have chattered my wolf shifter's ear off just like anyone else.

Actually, that might have been fun to watch.

Several more feline kin from the prominent families joined us at the head table. I found myself facing a cheetah pair, the wife rubbing her cheek with the back of her hand like a house cat washing its face. Next to them was a pair of lions that included the woman who'd greeted me so skeptically when I'd first arrived. Coreen—that was her name. My head was getting awfully crowded with those.

Thankfully, Julius was sitting nowhere near us. I spotted his hulking form at the far end of the room, where I guessed Marco had asked his attendants to put him. And I wasn't exactly disappointed to see Silvan stationed at a distant table too.

Marco's kin eyed him with darting glances as they dug into their meals. They ate like cats too, with swift delicate bites. Coreen dabbed at her mouth with her napkin after every forkful.

"Is the challenge arena already prepared?" she asked after a few minutes of strained silence. It was weird how a question that ominous could be said as if it was a polite inquiry. Her tone was the same as if she were asking what we were having for dessert.

But then, Marco acted equally unfazed. "My attendants are setting everything in order right now. I suppose you'll be there for the show."

"The more witnesses, the more worthy," Coreen's husband put in with a rumble of a voice.

"Interesting philosophy," West muttered.

Coreen shot him a hard look. Marco twitched under the table, and I suspected he'd just kicked the wolf shifter in the shin. His smile stayed pleasant.

"I'm glad the matter with the vampires up north was finally settled," the cheetah man put in. "There haven't been any more stirrings, have there?"

"Not of enough concern that my people up there have mentioned it to me," Marco said. "You know what the bloodsuckers are like. No attention span for anything unless it's actively bleeding."

The cheetah shifter woman snickered at that. My stomach had clenched tighter. "Was there a lot of trouble because of our confrontation with the vampires when we went into the city?"

Mom had left me a trail of clues leading to the mountain in Sunridge, and we'd had to go exploring the New York City subway system to find the first one. Right into vampire territory. They hadn't been real pleased about our intrusion.

Marco waved his hand. "Oh, just normal vamp mutterings. We sorted them out. They don't *really* want to tango with the shifters."

I wasn't sure how much that comment was the truth and how much was necessary bravado for his kin. Right now he probably needed to look strong and in control even more so than usual.

Aaron set his hand on my thigh under the table and squeezed reassuringly. He leaned close. "Tonight will be fine. Marco's been through this situation more than once. We all have. And we're still here."

I'd have felt more comforted if I hadn't sensed the worry underlying his words. He wasn't completely confident either. The rogue's involvement was a wild card none of my alphas had faced during a challenge before.

The talk all along the table quieted at the scrape of chair legs. A guy at the far end of the table had just stood up. He raised his hands with a smile that looked weirdly giddy. His hair, mixed with patches of dark brown and pale gray, poked up in tufts from his rounded head. I didn't remember being introduced to him earlier, but his appearance immediately made me think *snow leopard*.

"With all the commotion, I want to speak up and say how much I support our alpha," he said in a jovial voice that carried through the room. "Marco has kept us in line and seen us through troubled times no other alpha has had to address. I know he'll continue to do so."

He focused his gaze on his alpha and dipped into a

low bow. Marco chuckled, smiling back, but the guy's demeanor made my skin tighten. He seemed *too* eager to speak. Praising Marco more to ingratiate himself than because he meant it.

Was this some kind of attempt to protect himself? Did he think Marco would punish people who seemed at all in favor of Julius after he won? That didn't seem like the feline way of doing things.

Marco didn't appear bothered. "Thank you for your kind words, Phillipe," he said, holding up his glass as if to toast the leopard shifter. "I know it too. And in an hour, this whole room will know it."

CHAPTER 17

Ren

My heart started to thump harder the moment we reached the challenge area. It wasn't really anything more than a glade in the tropical forestland, a stretch of open grass maybe twenty feet in diameter surrounded by thick foliage. But Marco's people had clearly prepared it, as he'd said they would.

The grass was trampled flat as if the ground had been pounded as smooth as possible. A green smell like a fresh-mowed lawn hung in the air. A rope hung across the trees around the ring, separating the spectating area from the fighting turf. Lamps hung from a few of the branches, casting an eerie yellow glow over the space. The one near us emitted a soft electronic hum.

Marco walked ahead of me, right into the ring. Kylie and I drifted to the side, the other alphas and Alice surrounding us. Nate rested his hand on my shoulder. "If it's too hard for you to watch," he started.

I shook my head before he could continue. "I'm staying. I need to be here for Marco."

More feline shifters gathered all around the glade. It looked like everyone who'd been at the dinner had come. Why not? The leadership over their kin group might change tonight.

"Where's the tiger?" Kylie asked, craning her neck. "Maybe he chickened out at the last minute?"

Before I could even dare to hope, Julius came swaggering down the path. He sauntered into the ring across from Marco, flexing his bulky arms. Marco watched him calmly. With a casual ease, he pulled off his shirt, then his pants, folding his clothes one piece at a time on the ground at the edge of the glade. Julius bared his teeth and started undressing as well. Of course, they'd fight as animals.

I looked around the ring at all the faces I recognized. Coreen and her husband, the cheetah shifters from dinner, Silvan and the over-eager snow leopard Phillipe, others I'd met during the luncheon. None of them, not even Phillipe after his impassioned speech, looked all that concerned about what was going to happen. The vibe in the air now was swelling with anticipation.

Were they all sure Marco would win, or did they just not care that much either way who was ruling over them? From what I'd seen of the feline kin so far, I didn't have any trouble believing it might be the latter.

Kylie must have been thinking along the same lines. "Imagine having that musclehead as an alpha," she whispered to me. "I wouldn't trust him not to spend all day chasing his own tail."

My mouth twitched. I wasn't so tense that my bestie couldn't get a smile out of me. "No kidding. They'd be begging to have Marco back in no time."

Except he wouldn't be around for them to bring him back, would they? My pulse sped up even more.

I hadn't asked Marco what happened to *him* if he lost. I hadn't wanted to take the possibility that seriously. Would they banish him like they'd banish Julius? Or was the punishment of losing after you were already alpha more severe? The new alpha wouldn't want to risk you coming back to reclaim your position.

A chill trickled through me. Suddenly I was sure of it. If Marco lost, Julius would kill him. Maybe that was the only way Julius could win.

"The guards are still watching the edges of the estate, aren't they?" I said to my alphas.

Aaron nodded. "I was there when Marco gave the orders."

Alice gave me a meaningful look. "If you want the extra security, I could fly around and watch for any groups on the move heading this way."

A tiny bit of the tightness inside me released. "Yes," I said. "Please. And come back the second you see anything concerning."

She nodded and slipped away between the trees. Clothes rustled off, and her eagle form leapt up through the branches. I watched her disappear against the darkening sky.

"I don't know what they might have planned," West said. "But I haven't seen or scented any rogue presence nearby."

"Neither have I," Nate put in. "Maybe this *is* their plan. They're staking everything on Julius defeating Marco."

I frowned. "That doesn't make sense to me. They've never played by the rules before. There's got to be something more to it. But maybe the challenge is a separate part of the plan. Maybe Julius wanted to get that over with, to prove himself in front of his kin, before he has the rogues take on the rest of us."

Whatever happened, I needed to be ready. And I'd need to protect Kylie too. I edged a little closer to her. "If things get crazy, you stay with me, all right?"

She saluted me. "Got it, dragon queen."

The smile tugged at my lips again. Then I looked into the ring, and any humor I'd been capable of feeling died.

One of the estate attendants had stepped into the middle of the glade between Marco and Julius. "A challenge for alpha has been called," she said in a ringing voice. "When my arm drops, the fight may begin."

She held her hand up as she backed up to the ring of rope. When her back hit it, her hand clenched. She jerked it down to her hip in one sharp movement.

Julius sprang with a growl that was half human, half animal. His body shifted into tiger form as he lunged through the air at Marco. But Marco was prepared. He shifted and dashed low under the larger cat, spinning to scratch at the tiger's belly as he slid out of reach. Julius roared. Four thin red lines formed against his fur.

"First blood!" someone in the audience hollered. Someone else let out a whoop. I assumed that was good for Marco. My hands had closed around the rope in front me, the coarse fibers digging into my skin.

"Wow," Kylie murmured. "They really aren't playing around."

No, they weren't. Not at all. Julius whirled around, still plenty fast despite his size. My gut sank, seeing just how much bigger he was than Marco now. The tiger had to be at least twice as brawny as the jaguar, taller and longer and more solidly built. If he pinned Marco even for a second...

That was obviously Julius's intention. He leapt at Marco again, swinging a paw as if to cuff his alpha. Marco dodged to the side, not quite in time. The tiger's claws raked over his haunch. He didn't make a sound, but I saw his lips curl back in pain. I gripped the rope tighter.

"So... how far exactly do they go?" Kylie said in a smaller voice than before. "How do we decide when someone's won?"

"When one of them can't get back up," West muttered.

I swallowed hard. Murmurs were rippling through the crowd again. Were they upset that Marco hadn't really fought back yet?

He must have been working up to it. Feeling out his opponent's style before he took the offensive. Before Julius could make another lunge, Marco dashed at him with a yowl. The tiger lurched forward to try to batter the jaguar into submission, but that was exactly what Marco had expected. At the last second, he darted around the bigger cat and lashed out at Julius's belly again.

The tiger was moving forward with too much

momentum to dodge. Marco's claws opened a deep gash in Julius's side.

A nice bluff. Of course, if Marco was going to win here, he had to put on a front, prey on the larger shifter's confidence. That was the cunning his kin were supposed to be known for. And none so much as their alpha.

It wasn't so different from how he'd bluffed about his attitude toward me to his kin, put on a front of seeing me as nothing more than a means to an end. But I knew with every thud of my pulse that he'd used those words the same way he'd made that mad dash. A distraction, a show of force, to open up the way to what he really wanted. When this kind of hostility was what he'd had to face, month by month, I wasn't sure I could even blame him anymore.

Julius whipped around, his yellow eyes flashing. Marco sprang nimbly out of the way. But the tiger didn't seem slowed down by the gouge over his ribs. He hurtled after the jaguar like a Mack trunk, and Marco couldn't keep out of the way quite fast enough. The larger shifter bowled him over.

I flinched, my heart thumping so fast I thought it would explode from my chest. A scream caught in my chest. *No!* Not my alpha. Not my mate.

Nate set his hand over mine, squeezing my fingers, but the contact barely registered. I couldn't pull my eyes from the fight.

Marco rolled onto his back, all four sets of claws scraping at the tiger's hide. Julius smacked him in the head and snapped at his neck, but the jaguar twisted out of the way and the last second. He sank his teeth into the tiger's foreleg. When Julius flinched, Marco shot out from under him. He flung himself toward one of the trees, ricocheted off the trunk, and slammed into the tiger's side right where he'd clawed him before.

Julius let out a snarl that was as much pain as anger. He charged after Marco, clearly aiming to pummel him to the ground again. Marco slipped around him, but he wasn't moving quite as fast now. Blood dripped from where the bigger cat had clawed his shoulder and haunches.

"Geez," Kylie said, even more faintly. "They're really taking this to the end, aren't they?"

The fear in her voice wrenched at me, as much as seeing Marco battered and bloody did. Every nerve in my body was shrieking at me to intervene, to protect my mate. I held myself back by the barest of threads. If I stepped in, if I messed up this challenge somehow, the victory might go to Julius by default.

I wouldn't let him kill Marco. Not if it came to that. I knew that much right down to my bones.

Marco picked up his speed again despite his wounds. He raced around Julius, biting and clawing at the tiger's legs at every opening, leading the tiger in a whirling chase around the arena. Julius pounded after him. With each turn, his orange and black fur darkened with more streaks of blood.

"All right! Let's end this!" someone hollered from the crowd. I didn't know which of the shifters he was supporting.

For a moment it seemed like Marco was gaining the upper hand. Then his pace started to lag. He nipped the tiger's hind leg and barely scrambled out of the way of Julius's smack. But the tiger kept coming, his lips curled back over his huge fangs. The jaguar stumbled, and Julius pounced. Marco tumbled under him.

A cry broke from my throat then. My hands flinched where I was gripping the rope. Aaron's arm came around me, holding me steady as Nate held onto me too.

Marco lay, his black-furred body limp, under the tiger's huge form. Julius raised his head with a victory roar—and the jaguar leapt up. Marco caught the tiger by the neck, sinking his teeth in deep around the most tender point of his opponent's throat. At the same time, he kicked out at one of Julius's legs.

All his scratches and bites and the strain of running around the arena must have weakened the tiger's muscles. The bigger cat toppled over, Marco rolling with him. The jaguar came to rest poised on Julius's vulnerable chest. He raked his claws over the paler fur there and yanked at the tiger's throat.

Julius's eyes rolled back. He heaved at the ground, but Marco held on tight, managing to keep him pinned.

My breath had stopped in my lungs. I let it out in a rush. A cheer rose up around the ring. "Marco! The alpha wins!"

Marco sank his teeth even deeper with a low growl of warning that was almost a question. The tiger's head swayed as if he couldn't quite find the will to keep it off the ground. Then Julius slumped down, his body sagging. The shift rippled through him. Marco sprang off as the tiger turned back into a man.

The cheers grew louder, the crowd whooping and

clapping hands. A few of the waiting attendants darted into the arena to tend to the unconscious Julius's wounds. And to their alpha. Marco listed a bit to one side, blood smearing the grass under his paws—and plenty of it was his own. He pushed off the ground and shifted back into his human form, raising his hand in victory.

The tension in me broke, relief rolling through me. I raised my voice with a cheer of my own.

CHAPTER 18

Nate

"How long have you been in league with the rogues?" I said, barely managing to keep the growl out of my voice.

Julius slumped silent in his chair in the small room, his neck still marked with red where Marco had bitten him yesterday night. The wounds had healed but left behind scars that wouldn't fade for months, if not years. The tiger shifter had resisted forfeiting the challenge until he'd been on the verge of dying.

Marco, standing next to me, had scars of his own. Even after a night's rest, his movements were still a little stiff. I'd volunteered to help him lead this interrogation after I'd seen him at breakfast. And I might have had ulterior motives as well.

Someone had sent the rogues to corrupt my kin. I wasn't leaving here without finding out how—and who else they might have turned.

"How long?" I repeated. The other alphas and Ren

stirred where they were watching behind us. Julius swiped his hand across his mouth, the chain that linked his restraining cuffs clinking. He thought a lot of himself, all big and posturing, but he had nothing on me. I loomed over him, letting him think about what it'd be like to take on an animal more his own size.

"Since we got the news that the dragon shifter had been found," the traitor said in a reluctant voice. "Not long."

"So you admit that you've conspired with them?" Marco said.

The tiger shifter inclined his head slightly.

"You gave *them* orders? Was it your idea to send them to attack the disparate estate?"

"I thought it would be better if you were all dead," Julius said. "I might have given some advice about how they could manage that. I've been here on the estate the whole time, though."

"You sent them after *my* people," I snapped. "What did you tell them to say to my kin to persuade them to help? The rogues wouldn't have come up with any argument strong enough on their own—I know they couldn't."

"Oh, it wasn't that hard," Julius said with a twitch of his hand on his lap. He didn't look up at me. "Sweet talk them a little, give them the idea they'd be better off without some boss alpha running the show."

No. It had to be more than that. The answer set my teeth on edge. But maybe it was only because I didn't want to admit that my kin might be so easily swayed? Suddenly I was unsure of my judgment.

"You expect me to believe that's it?" I said, letting my voice rumble louder. "Exactly what were the rogues supposed to offer my kin that would be better than what they already have?"

Julius shrugged, his head still bowed. "What makes you think they have it so good right now?"

That wasn't an answer at all. I bristled and caught myself, taking a step back before I swung at him.

It wasn't an answer, and it also was. My kin *had* been swayed. Maybe the how didn't matter so much. They had their weaknesses, as much as I hated to admit it. But I had to admit it if I was going to address those weaknesses and help them get through whatever trouble lay ahead of us.

Because we were obviously far from done with that trouble.

"We know you had something planned with the rogues for our visit here," Marco said. "Care to share any details or should your dragon shifter burn the truth out of you?"

Ren came up beside me, wrapping her hand around my arm. She'd felt my distress. I didn't want to show any of my own weakness in front of our prisoner, but I did let myself quickly nuzzle her hair. The softly sweet smell of my mate steadied me.

"I just told them you were coming," Julius said. "That it would be a good time to get involved. That's all."

"Well, I definitely don't believe *that*," Marco said. He glanced at Ren. "Princess?"

Ren looked up at me as if asking my permission. As if she needed to. I could stand back for a moment. It might be better if I did. Instead of pushing for the answers I wanted, I needed to listen.

She'd gotten through to Orion. Maybe there was something redeemable in this wretched feline shifter too.

~

Ren

I came to stand directly in front of Julius. He kept his head low as if he thought he could worm his way out of telling the truth that way. Hadn't he heard the stories about my powers?

I wasn't going full dragon on him yet, though. He'd given me a strange vibe all through his questioning. I wanted to get a better sense of it.

"Look at me," I said. When he didn't move, I repeated the words with a hint of fire creeping into my voice. *"Look at me."*

The tiger shifter startled, his head jerking out. He blinked as his gaze met mine. His light brown eyes looked oddly hazy. There was no reason for him to be spaced out. He'd been complying enough so far that Marco hadn't had him drugged. If he tried to shift, the chains that bound him would hold his tiger form even more tightly.

"Tell me exactly where you met with the rogues," I said. "If it's been different places, start from the first time."

"I—I've only talked to them in person once," he said.

"Out beyond the glade. The other times, I had people speak for me."

I frowned. My senses told me he was telling the truth. But at the same time his whole demeanor, the vagueness of his answers, unsettled me.

"You could show us the spot?"

"I'm not sure I remember exactly where it was," he said. That seemed to be the truth too.

I ran my tongue over my teeth. "Who spoke for you the other times?"

"No one here. It was their idea. I couldn't tell you their names."

"We can make you tell us," Marco broke in. "And believe me, I'll very much enjoy watching you taken over by those flames."

I made a motion with my hand, and he stopped, his forehead furrowing. But Julius still gave every appearance that he was being truthful. My violet fire couldn't provoke more out of him than that.

If I got any clear answers, the most important questions were about what waited ahead, not what had already happened.

"Do the rogues plan to attack the feline estate?"

"I don't know," Julius said honestly. His lips curled slightly. I couldn't tell if he was on the verge of smiling or grimacing. A prickle ran down my back.

"Do they have anything planned for when we leave the estate?"

"I don't know."

"What *do* you know about what the rogues are planning to do next?"

The tiger shifter's head sagged back down. He let out a rough sigh. "I don't know anything about what they have planned next. As far as I'm concerned, they do a great job figuring out how to mess with you themselves."

"And what do you think they'd have done if you *had* managed to beat me?" Marco asked. "They're against the whole system of alphas. Did you really think they'd bow down to you after you'd become what they hate about the shifter kin?"

"I don't care," Julius said. "I just wanted *you* gone."

"Why?" Aaron asked from the back of the room. "What were you hoping to gain?"

Julius hesitated. Something about that question seemed to have thrown him off. His fingers curled over his knees. "Respect," he said. "Power. A better position than I have now."

All true. I bit my lip. Nothing he was telling us was any use, no matter how honest he was being.

I tipped my head toward the door. The alphas filed out, Marco lingering to shoot one last glare at his rival. I followed them. Marco closed the door behind us.

"Are we taking him outside so you can work your dragon magic on him?" West asked in his usual gruff voice.

I shook my head. "It wouldn't do any good. He's not lying to us. He's not being very clear, and there's something strange about the way he's answering, but the things he says he doesn't know... He really doesn't know them. Unless he's somehow strong enough to confuse my impressions when not even the four of you can manage that."

Marco smiled crookedly. "That hardly seems likely."

"It doesn't," I agreed. "But where do we go from there? He's admitted to working with the rogues, even if he doesn't seem to be half as involved as Orion thought. He seemed sure there was a feline calling a lot of the shots."

"Orion wasn't really in a position to give you many details," West pointed out.

"I don't like the idea of that one walking free," Nate said, jabbing his thumb toward the door. "If you simply banish him like a regular failed challenger, of course he'll go straight to the rogues. And who knows what plans he'll make with them then? He knows your estate; he knows your people. He'll tell them everything."

"There are other considerations," Aaron said.

"Like what?" the bear shifter demanded.

"Like how much I want to tell my kin about Julius's involvement with the rogues," Marco put in. "If I imprison him instead of banishing him, I'll have to explain it somehow. And they might not even believe it. For all they know, I'm making up an excuse after the fact to justify tormenting him further. Which won't exactly do wonders for morale around here."

Shit. I hadn't thought of that. I crossed my arms over my chest. "So what's our best option?"

Marco sighed. "I don't know. I can keep him confined a little longer without too many questions, but I'll need to make some kind of official move soon. Now would be an excellent time for my feline cleverness to kick in."

"We'll all think on it," Aaron said.

Unlike on Nate's estate, the holding cells on Marco's

weren't in a basement but a separate building off to the side of the main mansion. When we stepped out, Kylie and Alice were waiting for us.

Kylie bounded to my side, but her face still looked a bit drawn. She'd been quieter since the challenge fight yesterday. That was part of the reason I'd wanted her to stay out here while we did the questioning.

"So what did you find out?" she asked, her gaze flicking back toward the building we'd left.

"Not much," I said. "We still have no idea whether the rogues are going to attack us here, and if they are, how."

"Was he really helping them?"

"It seems like it. He admitted to it."

Kylie cocked her head. "What happens to him now, then?"

I spread my hands. "From what the guys have told me, usually a failed challenger would be banished. His kin mark would be stricken, and they'd mark him on the forehead where anyone could see to show his new status." I gestured to my own forehead. "Any kin who saw him anywhere near kin territory would have license to kill him. And..."

My voice faltered when I noticed Kylie's expression. Her face had taken on a slightly sickly cast that clashed pretty awfully with her pink pixie cut. She glanced at me in my sudden silence and smiled, but her mouth wobbled.

Here I was talking about people getting killed like it was nothing. No wonder she was feeling ill.

"Are you okay?" I asked. "If you need anything..."

Kylie laughed awkwardly. "No, no. I think I've just had enough shifter brutality for a few days. I didn't sleep that well last night. Maybe I'll take a nap."

"I can see you back to your room," Alice offered. I was about to jump in and say I would, but I caught myself. Maybe it was me Kylie needed some distance from as well as the rest.

I looked around with a knot in my gut. My mates had ambled toward the mansion too. Marco had fallen a little behind the others, his expression uncharacteristically solemn. He didn't look worn down exactly, but his usual sly energy had dulled.

The challenge yesterday had clearly taken more out of him than he liked to admit.

I caught up with him, slipping my arm around his elbow. He brightened when he looked at me. "Hello, princess."

I tipped my head against his shoulder. Suddenly all I wanted to do was wrap myself up in his warmth. Revel in the fact that he was still here, living and breathing, not lying broken under that tiger shifter's paws.

"I feel like we both need a little more recovery time after last night," I said. "Is there somewhere on the estate we can at least pretend to relax? Maybe that's what you need to get those cleverness juices flowing."

The corner of Marco's mouth quirked up. "Actually, I know just the place."

CHAPTER 19

Ren

WITH ALL THE COMMOTION YESTERDAY, I hadn't gotten the chance to explore much of the house yet. When Marco opened the door into the vast greenhouse I'd only seen from outside, my breath caught.

"Wow." I stepped onto the stone path that wove into the thick tropical underbrush. Overhead, trees jutted limbs in an arching canopy. Artificial cliffs had been carved out of rock here and there along the walls, offering climbing ledges at various levels. The air was warm and humid but not stifling. A floral perfume drifted around me.

"It's like your jungle gym back at the New York house, only ten times bigger," I said.

"That's the idea." Marco took my hand, and we headed together down the path. "The climate might be warmer here in Florida, but the winters are still cooler than many of us prefer. And this gives us space to exercise our feline natures without any worries about being observed. A wolf or a bear can get away with running around in the woods without too much caution. A jaguar or a lion? That'd draw some attention if any humans spotted us."

No kidding. "I don't suppose there's a *really* big one of these out at the dragon shifter estate?" I said. "Because if a big cat is noticeable..."

Marco chuckled. "Your home base is in an isolated enough spot that you can fly near there without any problems. The dragon shifters have accumulated a lot of property in the surrounding area to keep humans at a distance."

The temperature hadn't felt too warm when we'd first stepped in, but a sheen of sweat was forming on my skin now. I rubbed my arms. "Too bad you can't turn the temperature *down* if you need to."

"There are other ways to cool off," Marco said slyly. "Shedding clothes is always my favorite."

I shot him a mock glower. He grinned back, looking more like his usual self. At least that part of my plan was working.

"Actually," he said with a tug of my hand, "I think I have just the thing to convince you..."

We ducked through a passage formed by an arching bush and came out on the edge of a manufactured pond. Water burbled into it from a spout at one end. The walls and base were painted brown to look like soil and the vegetation grew right up to the edges, but the water was crystal clear. And it looked delightfully inviting.

"Hmm," I said. "You make a compelling case."

"I'm going in even if you're not," Marco replied, still grinning. He stripped off his shirt in a single movement and undid his pants. Damn. The casual air with which shifter guys got naked was starting to seem normal to me, but it was still fucking *hot*. In the best possible way.

And I was still hot, in a not-so-great way, standing here in my clothes. It wasn't as if Marco hadn't seen me naked a dozen times already.

I yanked off the cotton dress I'd managed to find among the fancier offerings in my wardrobes. Marco made an approving sound and leapt into the pool. A little of the spray dappled my skin as I wriggled out of my panties. The droplets felt so beautifully cool that I didn't stop to test the water. I just plunged right in after him.

The pond was deep enough that my head went under before my feet touched the bottom. I pushed myself back to the surface, reveling in the rush of the water against my skin. I'd never actually gone skinny-dipping before. Now I was thinking I'd need to make a habit of it.

I flipped my wet hair back from my face. Marco beamed at me, his own hair shining like black ink.

"There are ledges along the banks," he said. "If you get tired of treading water."

"I think my legs can handle a little treading."

"Hmm. Just be careful of the eels."

"What?" I jerked up, peering into the water below me.

Marco cracked up. "I'm teasing, Princess. I solemnly swear the entire estate is eel free."

"You..." I couldn't find the words to express what I

thought of that joke, but that was fine. I had a whole pool of water to work with. I aimed a splash right at his face.

Marco's eyes gleamed. "Are you sure you want to go there? Don't start a battle you're not prepared to lose."

"Big talk from a wet cat," I retorted, and splashed him again for good measure.

He wiped his face with a playful growl. "You asked for it."

Instead of splashing me back, he sprang at me. I squealed and dove out of the way. I managed to get in one more splash before he caught me by the waist. With his other arm, he scooped up a heap of water and dropped it right over me.

I shook my head, sputtering a laugh, and squirmed out of his grasp. The kick of my legs sent a good spray back at him. Then Marco snatched my ankle. "Hey!" I protested as he reeled me in.

"Look what I caught," he teased. "A rare dragon fish."

In a stunning show of maturity, I stuck my tongue out at him and kicked up another wave with my other leg. Marco tugged my ankle past him, surging forward at the same moment to grab my wrists. He pinned them gently against the side of the pool. "That's enough of that."

My feet came to rest on one of those ledges he'd mentioned. "You're no fun," I told him.

"Oh," he said, his voice dipping lower as he eased closer, "you have no idea how much fun I can be."

I snapped into sudden awareness of the rest of his body, just inches from mine in the water. His very naked body. *My* very naked body ached with the longing for him to cross those last few inches. I held his gaze, warmed by the heat in his indigo eyes.

"I don't know," I said, my own voice dropping. "I think I've gotten a pretty good idea. But you're always welcome to give me another demonstration."

"A very tempting invitation," he murmured.

He bent his head, and I tipped mine to meet his kiss. His mouth was slick and hot, demanding enough to send a tremor of desire through me. I wanted to touch him, to run my hands over that sleekly muscled body and pull it against mine, but he held himself away from me and kept my wrists locked in place. All I could focus on was the kiss.

His tongue slid into my mouth, and mine rose to tangle with it. A needy whimper crept up my throat as the kiss deepened. I was drowning in it, in the faintly spicy taste of him, in the craving for more.

Marco released my mouth to trail his lips down my neck. My eyelids fluttered open. My gaze caught on a stark red mark that ran from behind his ear down the base of his scalp. I winced, my heart stuttering with an emotion that had nothing to do with arousal.

Marco pulled back. "What's the matter?" he asked, his eyes concerned. His grip on my wrists loosened.

I drew back one of my hands to touch the side of his neck. My thumb traced over the fresh scar. "I didn't realize Julius got you here." So close to his throat.

"It doesn't really matter, does it?" Marco said lightly. "I'm the one who got him in the end."

"I know." But the fear I'd felt during their fight echoed through me. "I hated watching the two of you," I said in a small voice. "Every time he hurt you, I felt it too. You have no idea how much I wanted to leap in there and go dragon ballistic on his ass."

I finished that sentence with a growl. Marco smiled. "That would have been a sight to see. Maybe you'll still get a chance, the way things are going."

I didn't want to think about that—about the rogues and the threat still looming over us. That huge problem would be right there waiting for us when we left the greenhouse. For now...

Lowering my head, I pressed my lips against the scar. Marco's breath hitched. His heart thumped under my hand where it rested against his chest. I kissed every inch of the ruddy line that had been just a hair's breadth from a fatal wound.

A light that was almost wild shimmered in Marco's eyes when I drew back. He leaned in, close enough that his nose brushed mine. His voice came out slow and almost choked.

"I meant what I said before. About wanting you more than I want to be alpha. When I was facing him, that was all I thought about. Beating him so I could stay your mate. Being able to kiss you again. Being able to laugh with you again." He paused, pulling back again so he could meet my gaze. "My Princess of Flames. My Serenity. My dragon shifter. No matter what else happens, there's never going to be anyone else for me. I love you, Ren."

My throat had gone tight. Emotion swelled in my chest, bright and heady. "I love you too," I said without even needing to think about it. It was almost a relief to say it. God, why hadn't I already, to all of the guys? I needed to, more. All of the time. Until they couldn't possibly forget it. Because it was true. In the midst of all the chaos, I'd fallen for them with every bit of my heart.

The same rush of feeling flowed back to me from everywhere Marco and I touched. He grinned at me, so brilliantly I almost lost my breath. He moved as if to kiss me again, but at the same moment voices carried from the other end of the greenhouse.

"What do you think, trees or ground?"

"Why not both? I could use a good run."

Shit. Of course, all the feline kin had free run of this place. I grimaced, and Marco shook his head, his smile turning wry. I was getting used to all the shifters seeing me unclothed, but I wasn't exactly keen to make this private moment with my mate suddenly public.

"When they see us together, they'll probably leave," Marco murmured.

A crazy idea lit in my head. One that would at least skip the seeing us part. And maybe would restore a little more of Marco's reputation with his kin. A mischievous smile crossed my lips. Marco raised his eyebrows, and I pressed a finger to his mouth to tell him to keep quiet. Then I raised my voice.

"Oh, Marco! Yes, just like that. Mmm, don't stop!"

The corners of Marco's eyes crinkled as he suppressed his amusement. The intruders' conversation fell silent. I threw in a loud moan for good measure. "Oh, yes. Give it to me hard! You're so good!"

There was a brief rustling, and then the thud of the door closing. Marco tipped his head next to mine, his shoulders quaking with muted laughter. A snicker slipped out of my mouth. We both burst into giggles.

I swiped the tears of amusement from my eyes. "How long do you think it'll be before they dare set foot in here again?"

"They'll probably wait until I'm halfway across the country," Marco said. "You're lucky they didn't happen to be eager voyeurs."

"Oh, I'm sure I could have come up with something else in that case."

His eyebrows shot back up. "Now I'm sorry I missed the opportunity to see that."

"Too bad for you." Or maybe not. His arm had come to rest just below my breasts. Our legs had intertwined on the ledge. My heart skipped, with nothing but desire now. "What do you think? Can you make me sound like that for real?"

Marco's gaze started to smolder. "I think I'm up to that challenge. Is that what you want, Princess?"

It was. In that moment, when he looked at me like that, there was nothing I wanted more.

"I want you," I said, low but clear. "All of you. Marco, will you take me as your mate?"

A guttural sound escaped him, and then he was kissing me again, with so much passion it set my body on fire. I gripped his shoulder with one hand, the other trailing down over the muscles I'd so longed to explore earlier. The water lapped around us as we claimed each other's mouths completely.

Marco brought his palms to my breasts, circling the heels of his hands against my nipples. The water teased them even harder between each of his caresses. I moaned against his mouth, arcing into his touch. He took the opportunity to tangle his tongue around mine. We dueled and devoured each other as his hands dipped. When he pinched my nipples between his thumb and forefinger, a spark of stark pleasure shot straight down to my core.

I gasped, my hips bucking against him. The hard length of his erection brushed my core, making me twice as hungry in an instant. He left my breasts to grip my thighs and pull me to him. His cock settled against my clit. I shuddered with pleasure as he rocked his hips, inflaming me more with every stroke.

"The answer is yes," he muttered. "In case there was any doubt about that." Then his mouth caught mine again. I floated on the bliss racing all through my body, but my sex throbbed with a deeper need.

I reached between us to curl my fingers around his cock. Marco hummed happily as I slid them up and down. I lifted my hips, offering myself to him, and his chest hitched again.

He pulled back from our kiss to meet my eyes. A question shone in his. As if I hadn't already made myself clear enough.

"Please," I said, drawing him forward.

He pressed me harder against the wall as he eased his cock into me inch by glorious inch. I clutched at him, resisting the urge to buck against him like a wild woman, no matter how much I wanted him all the way in, now. The thrilling burn radiated from my core through every nerve. He kissed the corner of my jaw as he plunged all the way to the hilt. His breath spilled hot down my neck.

"Oh, God, Princess," he groaned. "So fucking beautiful."

I panted, lost in my need for him. "Less talking, more fucking."

He chuckled roughly and started moving. With each thrust, my body trembled more, clamoring for release. Our bond flared between us with a rush of bliss that left me breathless. I pumped my hips in time with his rhythm, whimpering as he pushed even deeper.

"I don't have you screaming my name yet," he murmured. "That's what you asked for, isn't it?"

"This is good," I said raggedly. "This is—oh!"

He adjusted the angle of my hips with his next thrust. His cock pressed against that sensitive spot inside me with one long stroke. I quaked with the sensation, ecstasy blurring my vision.

Marco picked up his pace, hitting that spot with a heady caress every time. I moaned, my head falling back. "God. Right there. Don't stop."

His chuckle was lost in another groan. He plunged into me once, twice more, and that was enough to send me spinning over my peak. I cried out, loud enough that the whole room probably could have heard it if I hadn't already scared everyone else away.

Marco's lips collided with mine. I kissed him through the bursts of sparks going off behind my eyes. Then with a shudder he followed me over, spilling himself inside me.

He rocked to a stop, letting me ride out the aftershock. I hugged him, shivering with bliss. "Now that's my princess," he said softly. His arms came around me, returning my embrace.

I tucked my head against his shoulder, overwhelmed by more feeling than I could blame on the sex. "And this is my mate," I whispered back.

He kissed my cheek, running his fingers over my hair. I nestled closer to him. How much longer could we stay here? It had become such a beautiful escape.

Marco tipped back my head to claim my lips again. The kiss started out gentle, but as I returned it, fresh desire stirred inside me. He made an approving sound as I kissed him more deeply.

I was just thinking we might go for a second round—to make up for lost time and all—when a clatter carried through the greenhouse walls.

We both froze, ears perking. For a second, there was nothing. Then the air split with the *boom* of a gunshot.

CHAPTER 20

Ren

MARCO and I scrambled out of the pond. No time for clothes. No time to even try to dry off. Droplets trickled down my back and over my chest as we raced along the path toward the door. Any heat that had still been in me fled. All I felt was a chill piercing straight through the middle of my chest.

Another shot rang out, one that sounded as if it was coming from inside the mansion now. My muscles clenched. Memories flickered by in the back of my head. The clean pale halls of the dragon shifter home, splattered with blood. A sister, a father, another, sprawled on the floor. The click of a rifle being reloaded.

A coppery flavor rose in the back of my mouth. No. I wasn't going to witness another slaughter. The rogues wouldn't take my alphas from me. They wouldn't take any one of the kin here.

But the thud of my heart and the shots still

reverberating in my ears told me they most likely already had. And to barge onto the estate in the middle of the day, guns blazing, they must have had help.

Not from Julius. We'd left him locked in that holding room.

I glanced at Marco as we reached the door. "There's another traitor among your kin," I said. "That must be why Julius was being so dodgy. He really didn't know that much. He was someone else's puppet."

Marco jerked open the door. "So it seems," he said, his voice tight. "Which just means someone else here needs to feel my fangs in their jugular before the hour is over."

If he could get close enough before he took a bullet. My lungs clenched. I grabbed his arm. "We'll hurry, but we can't go rushing right in there. They have weapons. We don't. We'll have to be smart."

Marco shot me a sharp smile. "I know how to fight smart, princess. Don't you worry about me. Didn't you see me last night?"

He took my hand, squeezing it tight, and we ran together down the hall. Voices clamored and a scream echoed from up ahead. My nerves twitched to shift, to rain a furious fire down over everyone who threatened my kin, but I didn't dare give in yet. I needed to save every bit of that energy for the actual fight.

Marco didn't have the same concerns, though. He gave my fingers another squeeze and then let go. A second later, he was leaping forward in jaguar form. Within a few bounds, he'd completely outpaced me.

I couldn't let him run into the fray alone. I pushed my

legs harder, drawing on all the dragon strength I held even in my human body.

We turned a corner, and the main foyer with its expansive staircase came into view up ahead. A body was slumped at the base of the stairs. Three others ran past the hallway, their faces white with panic. A lion bounded forward and jerked to the side as one of the guns boomed. Blood boomed on his tawny shoulder.

"There's no point in fighting!" a vibrant voice called out. Something about it struck me with a twang of recognition. "We've got no quarrel with the regular kin. Bring forward the alphas and the dragon shifter, and the rest of you can go about your business as usual."

Another voice reached my ears from farther away: Nate's rich baritone. "Away into your rooms, feline kin," he was hollering. "Lock your doors. This is for us to deal with."

Were the other alphas already there too? My pulse stuttered. I threw myself forward even faster, the muscles in my legs burning. Marco dashed on ahead of me, his paws thumping against the heavy pile of the rug.

The lion charged again, even with its limp. The air crackled with gunfire. There was a thump out of my view, but I could imagine all too well what had happened: the great cat slumping and sinking back into his human form. Blood pooling under his slack body.

Another memory flashed through my mind, so sharp and stark I lost my sense of the hall around me. I was five, clutching my wolf father's arm. Sobbing so hard my stomach lurched. Hands tacky with blood. That click of the rifle. Then my mother's fingers snatching my arm and wrenching me to my feet.

Away. Away.

I stumbled, and suddenly the foyer was right there in front of me. The body I'd imagined lay just a short distance from my feet—Coreen's husband, his eyes unblinking. I jerked myself back against the wall.

Chaos reigned all around the staircase. The feline shifters hadn't listened to Nate's call, at least not most of them. Even in a crisis they apparently weren't willing to listen to a bear. Panthers and tigers, lions and lynxes, snarled and lunged at animal foes of all sorts beneath and on either side of the steps. Several other bodies were slumped in its shadow. I couldn't tell which were our people and which rogues. There seemed to be a hundred enemies battling us.

My alphas were in the middle of the fray, Nate's bear and West's wolf looking as though they were trying to urge the other shifters down the central hall while fending off the rogues, Aaron's eagle swooping around the stairs to tackle a weasel about to leap at the others from above.

Alice was there too—in human form, pushing Kylie behind her in one corner. My pulse hiccupped. I didn't know how they'd ended up in the room, but they were trapped now unless they ran through the fighting. My best friend braced her back against the wall, her arms hugged tight around herself. Her wide eyes were fixed on figures at the other end of the foyer.

Across the thick runner by the mansion's double doors, the rogues still in human form were standing. Two held pistols and three others rifles. They'd gathered more weapons than the other groups had carried for previous attacks. My gut twisted at the sight—and then twisted tighter when I spotted a familiar face in their midst as they marched forward.

I'd counted wrong. There were three pistols, but the guy holding the third wasn't a rogue. It was Phillipe, the patchy haired snow leopard shifter who'd made such a show of praising Marco last night.

As if he'd felt my gaze on him, his eyes darted to the side and found me. The woman beside him raised her rifle to take a shot at Aaron, clipping him in the wing. Phillipe smiled thinly and motioned to the others.

"There's our dragon shifter," he said, his jovial voice turned cruel. "Take her down."

Three of the guns snapped toward me. I threw myself back toward an open doorway down the hall. At the same moment, Marco hurtled forward.

The jaguar slammed into the nearest rogue, knocking her over just as she fired. The guy next to him flinched, his shot going wild. Phillipe swore and pointed his pistol at Marco.

"No!" I reeled forward again, pushing off the floor as I did. The shift ripped through me faster than it ever had before. My muscles screamed, and my skin stung. A stabbing pain shot through my bones. But I was there, with a draconic roar, plowing straight into Phillipe before he could pull the trigger.

Aaron dove at one of the other armed rogues. Nate came charging through the battleground to join us, West wheeling to follow. The rogue Marco had tackled slammed her gun against the side of his head and managed to roll out from under him. He caught her wrist with his jaws. With a yank and a cracking sound, she gasped. The pistol clattered to the floor.

Phillipe had toppled when I'd hit him. He shifted as he sprang away. I melted his gun with a blast of dragon fire and swung around to pursue him. Where was Kylie? I had to make sure she stayed okay. I had to try to keep *everyone* here okay.

The snow leopard crossed Nate's path, and the grizzly battered him to the side. All around us the battle raged on. One of the remaining human rogues fired a few more shots, one of them smacking Nate in the hip. Blood sprayed across the polished floorboards. Fur flew and animal voices shrieked. I could hardly tell which of the living bodies were my kin and which the rogues now.

In that glance, a hard certainty formed inside me. I didn't care if Nate's kin or Marco's had doubted my ability to lead them. I didn't care what the rogues might have offered them as an alternative. *This* was what the rogues brought. Violence, pain, mayhem. This was what they'd always brought.

Maybe I didn't know how good a leader I'd be, but I sure as hell could do better by my kin than this.

With the strength of that resolve coiled tight in my belly, I blasted the rogue who'd shot Nate with a spurt of flame. He screeched and crumpled. The rogue whose wrist Marco had snapped was struggling to grip her gun with her weaker hand. I charred her to cinders before she could get a handle on it.

West had charged at one of the guys who held a rifle.

The wolf snapped at the rogue's legs while the guy tried to swivel far enough away to aim. He'd already gotten in one shot—a streak of starker red slashed through the ruddy silver fur on West's back where a bullet had clipped him, only just missing his spine.

Rage flashed behind my eyes. I couldn't fry the rogue without frying my mate at the same time. But I had teeth and claws too.

I bashed the guy's head with a swipe of my foreleg. In an instant, West was on him, his teeth at the rogue's throat. He kicked the rifle aside. I shot a bolt of white hot flame down on it, turning it into a bubbling mass of metal.

A sliver of a thought passed through my head: Mom would have made short work of the rogues that had attacked her family sixteen years ago, if she'd been able to fight like this. If she hadn't had three daughters who couldn't fully shift to try to protect.

The people we loved, the ones who were weaker than us—they made us vulnerable.

Panic washed over me. Kylie! I leapt over the staircase, searching for her. Searching for the snow leopard who'd managed to scramble through the fray.

I found both of them. Phillipe was facing off against Alice, still in her human form, but no less dangerous for it. He lunged at her, and she rammed her elbow into the side of his skull. The blow sent him staggering to the side. Kylie yelped. She groped toward a painting hanging just beside her. Heaving it off its hook, she hurled it at their attacker.

The corner of the heavy frame smacked Phillipe square in the head. I breathed a gust of fire toward the snow leopard, but he leapt out of the way at the last second. His cry of pain told me I'd at least singed him. He bolted away under the staircase.

With a roar, I barreled into the chaos of the fight. My talons picked off a jackal here, a rogue bear there, and another intruder, and another. The feline kin not too injured to keep fighting closed in around the dwindling number of remaining rogues. Which was a good thing, because the strain of the extended shift was catching up with me, with an even deeper pain than usual. Because I'd called my dragon form over me so quickly?

I'd have to ask Aaron about that, I thought vaguely as I tossed one last rogue against the wall. My muscles were contracting, no matter how hard I tried to hang on. I collapsed onto the floor. My human hands slammed into the floor, my human knees knocking the polished hardwood.

Sucking in a breath, I shoved myself to my feet. My gaze caught on a hunched form under the stairs.

Phillipe. The snow leopard sat curled in on himself. His left foreleg and most of that shoulder was burned black. His teeth were bared as he panted through the pain. Only the faintest shiver of sympathy touched me.

All of the blood spilled here was because of him. Why? So he didn't have to listen to someone else telling him what to do? Because he thought he'd get some kind of glory among the rogues?

It didn't fucking matter. The only thing that mattered was that he never did it again.

I strode over to him, slowing as I got closer. Phillipe

snarled, but he clearly wasn't capable of putting up much of an actual fight.

One of the other feline shifters, a cougar, came up beside me. "Drag him out," I said to her. "Out where everyone can see."

The snow leopard growled, but he couldn't do more than squirm and wince as the cougar took him by the scruff of his neck. The larger cat dragged him out to where the noon sun streamed through the thrown open doors. I stalked after them. My jaw clenched.

The cougar let go of Phillipe and backed up a step. I loomed over the snow leopard, meeting his yellow-green gaze with a glare. From around the room, dozens of feline eyes fixed on me. And one pair of human eyes. Kylie gaped at me, her face still pale.

The thought of what she must think of me now sent a pang through my chest. But I couldn't let those worries distract me. What I did here mattered a hell of a lot.

So I'd better do it good.

"Phillipe," I said, pitching my voice loud. "You were kin, and you betrayed all the others you should have called kin. You brought all this destruction down on your alpha's estate, your shifter community." I swept my arm to indicate the entire foyer. "But I will give you a chance. Because I am not here to destroy if I can help it. So much of shifter kind has been broken by the rogues and kin like you. Will you help us rebuild it now? Or do you only care about wrecking things?"

Phillipe clung on to his feline form, his eyes narrowing. The muscles in his haunches bunched. I braced myself, feeling his intention. If that was how he wanted to end this, let them see him make the choice himself.

He threw himself off the floor with one final surge of strength, his jaws yawning as if to eat me whole.

My hand tingled as I drew a partial shift into my fingers. With the snow leopard's sour breath in my face, I slashed my dragon talons across his neck, severing his throat.

CHAPTER 21

Marco

That traitor, Phillipe, crumpled at Ren's feet with a gush of blood down his chest. My dragon shifter dodged backward, shaking her hand to withdraw her talons. As the snow leopard shifted back into Phillipe's stringy human form, her head whipped around. Her gaze locked with mine. A sudden worry shimmered in her eyes.

Why? Because she'd killed one of my kin? Good riddance to that piece of excrement. She'd been fucking glorious.

I rose up out of my jaguar form, ignoring the aches and pangs where I'd have new scars tomorrow. Then I brought my hands together and started to clap.

Around the room, my kin and the other alphas were gradually shifting back. Most of them joined my applause. Ren's head swiveled as she took in our response, looking startled and then, with a lift of her chin that made my heart swell with affection, owning it. Not a princess of flames anymore. The woman before me was every inch a queen.

I walked up to her and took her hand. "He got what was coming to him," I said in a low voice. "You were amazing, Ren."

I leaned in to kiss her, and someone gave an exhausted but still joyful whoop in the crowd. All of my kin had to feel it now—that my bond with my mate had been consummated, that their own desires could bring them new feline children after all these years. But that wasn't the only reason to celebrate.

Ren kissed me back hard, as if replenishing her strength through the meeting of our lips. I was happy to give anything she needed to take. She touched my cheek, finding the claw mark just below my eye that hadn't yet sealed. I shook my head to tell her not to fret about that. The wound only stung a little while I stood here next to her.

Then I turned to face my kin and raised our joined hands in the air in a gesture of triumph. "The rogues and the traitors among our kin have been put down. This is the security a dragon shifter brings us. A new age for us is about to begin. An age when shifters will work together against our enemies, and live and love without the shadow of violence hanging over us."

"Here's to the dragon shifter!" someone—I thought Silvan—shouted from our audience.

"To the dragon shifter!" a bunch of voices joined in. Some wary, some limping, but all bright-eyed, several of my kin slunk over to show their respects to Ren, as if they'd only just met her.

Better late than never. A smile crept over my face as I watched them bob their heads and press their hands to hers, murmuring words of gratitude and encouragement. No one here had ever seen a battle like this on our home ground before. And no one here had seen a dragon fight like Ren just had.

Even a cat could appreciate the strength she'd shown—and the mercy.

My gaze traveled away from her to those we'd lost despite my mate's courage and all of our best efforts. Coreen's husband, Raoul, had taken a fatal bullet to the chest. The rogues had dealt fatal blows to a few others in the fray. A couple of my attendants who'd rushed in to help had fallen and not gotten up. And there were many kin alive but too weakened from their wounds to stand.

Several more attendants had slipped into the room now that the chaos had settled. I motioned them over. "Bring our injured kin to the medical room, quickly. And we'll need to arrange a funeral for the dead." I paused. Not all of the dead. Phillipe had lost the right to that respect, and the rogues had never earned it to begin with. "The rogues we'll burn too, elsewhere."

They nodded and ran to follow my orders. Coreen had gone to kneel by her husband, resting her hand on his forehead, her shoulders slumped. "I'll help see to him," she said in a rough voice to the attendants who'd joined her. Her gaze found mine.

"I'm sorry," I said.

Her mouth twisted. "He fought well. He didn't know how to stand back. It wasn't his nature." She looked over my shoulder, toward Ren, and then back to me. "Thank you," she added. "Maybe we have gone too long without a dragon shifter."

"I have no intention of losing this one," I said, and she managed a hint of a smile.

I made my way back to Ren. Some of my kin were still clustered around her, fawning over her. She was holding herself straight, answering them all warmly, but I could sense the exhaustion in her. My mate had fought too many battles in the last few weeks.

I wrapped my arms around her from behind. Even with the pain of my healing wounds, the feel of her bare skin against mine was heaven. I pressed a kiss to her shoulder and murmured in her ear, "Shall I escort you back to your rooms? I can't imagine how big a break you need after all that."

Ren's lips twitched. She leaned into my embrace for a moment. But her eyes traveled across the room to where her human friend was standing.

"I think there are a few things I need to take care of before I get to do any resting," she said.

Ren

I walked over to Kylie tentatively, watching for any sign that I'd come close enough. She'd never seen my dragon form before, and her first time, all she'd seen me do was clobber rogues and fry them into cinders. And then I'd sliced open a guy's throat right in front of her.

She'd already been having trouble coping with the

violence she'd been faced with. And now I was right in the middle of it. Maybe she'd just want to head right home and never speak to me again.

My best friend saw me coming and moving forward to meet me. I stopped, letting her set the pace. To my surprise, she strode right up to me and threw her arms around me, not seeming to care that I was naked and a little bloody.

"Oh my God, Ren," she said. "I was so scared for you. But you were such a badass! Holy shit, those rogues didn't know what hit them, did they? Fucking assholes."

I hugged her back with a halting laugh. "You were scared for *me*? I was freaking terrified one of them would hurt you."

"Aw, I had my eagle bodyguard fending them off. No problems there. And I got in a couple hits of my own." A tremor ran through her body, but she sucked in a breath and kept her voice steady. "I mean it. You were amazing."

My heart felt as if it had cracked open. My own breath came in almost a sob. Kylie pulled back to stare at my face. "What's wrong?"

"I just— Maybe it was stupid. I've been so worried that this whole... well, everything would be too much for you." I waved to the remains of the battle around us. "It's not what the shifter community is usually like. At least, from what the guys have told me it isn't. But everything is such a mess right now. I don't want to have to fight, but I do have to. People are dying... You shouldn't have to deal with all that."

"Hey," my bestie said firmly. She gripped my shoulder until I met her eyes. "I don't have to. But I want to. The second F in BFF stands for forever, remember? How much shit did we get into and then back out of when we were in New York? So the stuff you're mixed up in now is a little scarier—fine. Maybe I need to take a step back sometimes, but I'm still in this with you." A grin broke over her face. "My best friend is a *dragon*. How many people can say that?"

I really laughed then, and squeezed her with another hug. "You're the best, Kylie. I'm sorry I was shutting you out."

"I get it," Kylie said gently. "Just don't do it again, you hear?"

When I let her go, we stepped to the end of the room. Kylie's gaze drifted over the wreckage. "So... we don't have to worry about any more of those jerks showing up, do we?"

"I don't think so. From what we heard, this was their last-ditch effort, all-in to take us down. Otherwise Phillipe wouldn't have shown his hand."

And we'd defeated them. The rogues were decimated now—the ones who'd wanted me and my alphas dead, at least.

My legs wobbled under me. I might have tipped back against the wall if a large hand hadn't caught my arm.

"Hey," Nate said, bending to kiss my temple. "The shift and the fighting took a lot out of you." He glanced at Kylie. "Do you mind if I borrow her and make her get some rest?"

"Please do," Kylie said with a sweeping gesture. She shot me a grin and a wink as the bear shifter ushered me away.

The other alphas were waiting in the hall. "What about the rest of your kin?" I said to Marco.

"Ah, they're pretty good at looking after themselves," he said in his usual languid tone. "I gave a nice little speech and passed out some orders. That should hold them over for at least a few hours." His expression turned more serious. "We'll have the funerals tomorrow."

"And luck willing, no more for a long time after that," Aaron remarked. He took my hand as we headed to my guest suite.

When we reached the door, the four guys followed me in. I crawled onto the bed, and they piled on around me. The morning's exhaustion was already catching up with me. I yawned and set my head on the pillow, surrounded by their warmth, and just like that, I was out.

I woke up, a little groggy and achy but feeling a lot more alive than before, to a streak of late afternoon sun drifting through the window. I stretched on the bed, and my mates stirred. Looking down at myself, I grimaced.

"Okay, I think a bath is in order before dinner."

Marco slid off the bed with a chuckle. "As much as I'd like to join you for that, I think I'd better touch base with my kin. But I *will* see you at dinner... and after?"

The lilt of his tone sent a flutter of desire through me. I pushed myself up to meet him, pulling him into a kiss. "Of course 'and after.'"

I'd already checked out the bathtub in the suite's bathroom. Like the bed, the circular tub was plenty big enough for five. Four should be a piece of cake. I turned the taps until the water was gushing out in a steamy stream. A handful of sea salt to make it nice and invigorating—perfect!

"I take it we're all invited?" Nate said, strolling in after me.

"The more the merrier. I'd like to think of it as a big, wet reset button in this visit. Good-bye, rogues! Hello, whatever the heck shifters usually do!"

"There's plenty of time for you to learn all of that," Aaron said. He slipped his arm around me and pressed his lips to my shoulder. "And I look forward to guiding you along the way."

"Hmm. Me too," I said with a suggestive waggle of my eyebrows that made him laugh.

As I plunged into the hot water, West finally emerged from the bedroom. He took in me already submerged and his fellow alphas climbing in after me, and shrugged. "Why not?"

Well, that was about as much enthusiasm as I could hope for from my wolf shifter.

The whisper of the water against my skin brought back the memory of the more pleasant activities I'd gotten up to this morning. My little interlude in the pond with Marco. All the fun that could be had while playing around in the water. I licked my lips, looking around at my mates. Then a deeper urge gripped my heart.

I could have lost any of them today. If one of them had been caught by the wrong bullet, like Coreen's husband had... Just the thought of it wrenched at me.

They needed to know just how much they meant to me.

I glided through the water over to Aaron. He smiled, reaching to cup my cheek. I settled on his lap and leaned in for a kiss. His other hand settled on my waist, his thumb stroking over my side as our mouths pressed together slickly. I was plenty hot and bothered already by the time I eased back. But I held myself a little away from him and gazed into his bright blue eyes.

"I love you," I said, the feeling of it rushing through me as if saying the words out loud had uncorked a whole new bottle of adoration.

Aaron's face lit up. He kissed me again, even more deeply this time. Then he said, with his lips just an inch from mine, "I love you, Serenity. Always."

I drifted from him to Nate beside him. The bear shifter welcomed me into his arms, already grinning. I snuggled into his embrace and kissed him hard, wanting him to feel how much this mattered to me. He rumbled in his chest, his fingers caressing my back. I touched the side of his face as I pulled away to meet his warm brown gaze.

"I love you."

"I love you too," he said. "Don't you ever doubt it."

I brushed my lips to his again. Then I turned. West watched me from the opposite corner of the tub. His body was tensed, but his dark green eyes looked softer than usual.

"Come here, Sparks," he said. "I might as well get my kiss."

Did he think he wasn't getting the rest? Well, maybe I wasn't totally sure either. It was a little hard to follow how I felt with all the push-pull between us. But if he was offering a kiss, he'd better believe I was going to take it.

I floated over to him, half expecting him to change his mind. Or to grab me and plant one on me so hungry it made my head spin.

He reached for me, easing his fingers around my wrist to tug me a little closer. He teased his other hand into my hair. We held each other's gazes for a moment, his strangely searching. A flutter passed through my chest. Then he drew me the rest of the way to him.

His mouth claimed mine with a tenderness I couldn't have been prepared for. His lips coaxed mine apart to deepen the kiss, and just like that, I was lost in him. Lost in the gentle passion of his embrace, lost in the smell that lingered on his skin as if he'd brought the forests of his home here with him.

This was the man I'd known my mate could be. The one I'd caught glimpses of in the rare moments when he let his guard down.

My head *was* spinning when he released me from that lip-lock. I stared at him for a second, catching my breath, my whole body aflame with both lust and a more heartfelt longing. I drew in a breath to say what I'd said to the others, what felt undeniably true now—and the door thumped in the other room.

As I swiveled around, Marco strode into the room. He was frowning, his eyes dark with concern.

"A few of the rogues escaped," he said. "Not so many that we'd need to worry about them on their own, but— my people's reports say they headed north. Straight toward a troop of vampires that just annexed my New York property and is now moving on from there. It looks like the rogues have even more allies than we realized. And they've just incited a full-scale paranormal war."

I groaned, tipping my head back against the cushion of the water. So much for resting. But the resolve I'd felt during the battle only hardened inside me.

"Fine," I said. "They've got no idea what they're getting into when they mess with a dragon. It's time to show *all* our enemies what a bad idea that is, once and for all."

ABOUT THE AUTHOR

Eva Chase lives in Canada with her family. She loves stories both swoony and supernatural, and strong women and the men who appreciate them. Along with the Dragon Shifter's Mates series, she is the author of the Demons of Fame Romance series, the Legends Reborn trilogy, and the Alpha Project Psychic Romance series.

Connect with Eva online:
www.evachase.com
eva@evachase.com

Made in the USA
Coppell, TX
14 June 2023

18005093R00132